PRAISE

The Hartford Atonement

"Gun violence is an issue for our times. Emil Scordato, a self-made billionaire, decides to take up the crusade to reduce violence. Though, like the Job of Scripture, he is met with loss and lack of support, he never loses his belief that he was called to bring the changes we seek. *The Hartford Atonement* accurately reveals the effect gun violence has on each of us and challenges us to be like Emil and take up his quest. May his hope for safer communities be our hope, too."

—Monsignor Robert Weiss, pastor emeritus, Saint Rose of Lima Parish, Newtown, Connecticut

"With rapid-fire prose, *The Hartford Atonement* takes dead aim at Congress's open and dirty secret: Lawmakers are more interested in getting reelected with the help of the powerful gun lobby than protecting constituents from ever-rising gun violence. Pushcart Prize–nominated author Philip Barbara's deeply researched story makes you want to scream, 'Wake up Congress. Do something!'"

—Thomas Ferraro, twenty-year Capitol Hill correspondent for Reuters and Bloomberg

"Emil Scordato's crusade in *The Hartford Atonement* typifies how successful members of the Wall Street community use their wealth to ease a societal ill, in this case trying to get assault weapons off the streets."

> —Jonathan Niles, retired New York Stock Exchange floor trader, Oppenheimer Securities

"Philip Barbara's *The Hartford Atonement* probes how survivors in a small town process shock and grief after a high school massacre and the risks a billionaire takes to atone for his investments in gun companies. A heart-wrenching story of altruism and faltering hopes. I couldn't turn the pages fast enough to see if Congress would finally do something to stop the slaughter."

> —John DeDakis, award-winning novelist, writing coach, and manuscript editor

The Hartford Atonement

by Philip Barbara

© Copyright 2024 Philip Barbara

ISBN 979-8-88824-497-5

All rights reserved. No part of this publication may be reproduced, stored in a retrieval system, or transmitted in any form or by any means—electronic, mechanical, photocopy, recording, or any other—except for brief quotations in printed reviews, without the prior written permission of the author.

This is a work of fiction. The characters are both actual and fictitious. With the exception of verified historical events and persons, all incidents, descriptions, dialogue and opinions expressed are the products of the author's imagination and are not to be construed as real.

Published by

3705 Shore Drive
Virginia Beach, VA 23455
800-435-4811
www.koehlerbooks.com

The Hartford Atonement

Philip Barbara

VIRGINIA BEACH
CAPE CHARLES

To my parents, the late Ann and Anthony Barbara,
and to every elected official and citizen who votes for laws
that in time cut gun violence by 25 percent.

1

MY GRANDSON JACK fell into a coma after being trampled by spectators escaping a man who was shooting up a high school gymnasium. We don't know if he'll ever wake up. The boy's trauma prompted his dad, Ted, a lifelong drunkard, to knock off a bottle of gin every day by 5 p.m., before turning to beer. The parade of services for the twenty dead began today with a Mass for our wrestling coach. Ted's wife, Mary, held his arm to steady him as he wobbled up the church steps. Kelly and I followed them, ready to help our son. People bundled in coats and scarves against the January cold streamed up and around us. Several gave me a knowing nod to assert grimly, "Emil Scordato, we're in this together."

One mourner broke the silence by calling out what I'd been thinking these past several days: "Where does the love of God go?" If pressed, I couldn't answer.

As we filed in, an Irish tenor's voice filled the church, singing "Fields of Gold." The Todd's Chapel school colors were displayed, and flower arrangements on vases and easels stood on each side of the altar. We walked up the center aisle. Mary carefully handed Ted off to a former teammate so that he could sit with the wrestling team that won the regional championship nineteen years ago; several members had come a good distance to pay their respects to Coach Brian Cleary. Kelly and I sat several rows behind them, and Mary joined us.

The coach was the intended target when the shooter stepped into the packed gym during a wrestling match and sprayed the bench with machine gun fire. In addition to the dead, another dozen were wounded. Many were hurt as they tumbled down the stands to escape. Jack, the only freshman on the team, was knocked to the gymnasium's hardwood floor and fell beneath the cascading feet.

As the tenor's final notes died away, the sounds of sobbing and coughing rose up, and Father Paul Rushmore began the Mass. I followed along but kept an eye on Ted. The men beside him stood as erect as Marines, but as we knelt and stood time and again, my son nearly buckled. I half expected him to lift a flask from his pocket; he had bottles stashed everywhere at his home. That first day after we visited Jack at the hospital, I should have driven around town with Ted to see other families stricken by the shooting, taken him to a Yale basketball game, or just sat with him, anything to keep him from drinking all day and into the evening. The gravity of the situation should have sobered him up instead of blinding him to our family problems.

When the priest began his homily, people ceased shifting in their seats. "Until now, Todd's Chapel had been an invisible town. It's a quaint and hospitable place, and if you were to go any distance, few people would know much about it. That has changed. Now it will be known everywhere as a place of terrible tragedy, like Columbine, Parkland, Uvalde, and our neighbor just up the road, Newtown." He spoke of gun violence like a war. "At the end of World War I, a *New York Times* correspondent in France wrote: 'Four years' killing and massacre stopped as if God had swept His omnipotent finger across the scene of world carnage and cried, 'Enough.' The combatants heeded His command and signed an armistice. So now I ask: Where is our armistice from such wanton killing? Where is our peace? There is none. Rather than listen to God, our leaders in Washington listen to themselves in one great echo chamber."

Kelly gently elbowed me and nodded in Ted's direction. "He's faltering. He better sit down."

"His friends will keep him upright."

After the benediction, the tenor sang "The Parting Glass," a gift to Coach Cleary's wrestlers as everyone began filing out. Mary caught up with Ted, and Kelly and I walked behind them to their car. He settled into the front passenger seat, and Mary drove off. I followed her home.

I was glad for a few moments of quiet on the short drive. Our son's drinking tormented Kelly, who swore Ted's alcoholism was hereditary. Her father was a drunk and died of a heart attack at fifty-nine. She had often expressed alarm about how Ted was heading toward that future. I was worried about Kelly too; she anguished over both Jack and Ted, so she wasn't sleeping at night. She looked haggard; her tall frame bent forward when she walked. But a sideways glance now revealed she appeared peaceful. Her hands rested on her purse in her lap, and she looked at the road ahead. Our concierge physician, Dr. Bertrand, had come around and, after a brief exam, had given her a prescription for her anxiety.

Our second child, Carol, was killed fifteen years ago when hit by a truck while cycling. We both felt that pain and how near it was again. I couldn't deny that, but I tried not to show it. After attending to Kelly, Dr. Bertrand said to me, "You also look terrible. How do you feel?"

"I feel the bottom has yet to drop out. Jack could die. Ted's in serious trouble." I told him about a scene at the hospital that had been especially unnerving. "I'm standing in the lobby when a woman who was crying uncontrollably shouted over the heads of everyone, 'Hey Mr. Scordato, what are you going to do about keeping this town safe?'"

"She's looking to people of stature for answers. That's natural."

"But I don't have special powers. I can't even protect my own family."

"You need to relax." As he wrote out the prescription for me, he said, "When I was a teenager, I attended an aunt's funeral. My uncle said to me that death is a door that opens to reveal the lives of a family. If that's true, a mass murder reveals the life of an entire community."

I considered this. Todd's Chapel was a small, quiet, well-to-do town northeast of Bridgeport. If a crow were to fly over the trees that cover the rolling hills of Connecticut, it would be forty-five miles from Hartford, the city where I grew up. Todd's Chapel retained its colonial charm because dozens of centuries-old homes had been restored. On Main Street, new street lamps with LEDs lined the red brick sidewalks. The bricks were reset last year. The town was home to a few Wall Street financiers like me. Once in a while, someone I knew sounded off about the wealth here. After a round of golf at the country club where I'm an investor, my partners and I would sit for dinner in the grill room. We played poker late into the evening and discussed everything, getting off on tangents and having round after round of drinks. One night, a guy asked in an offhand way, "Hey Emil, how much did you make last week?" As if wealth relieved me of all burdens.

We could hear Mary shouting at Ted as we came up the walk. Inside, Ted was fixing himself a gin and tonic. He slumped into a cushioned chair and took a long sip. Kelly and I took a seat. Ted's face sagged, but then he looked up: "I'm trying to imagine what the echo in the gym was like when that guy fired seventy rounds in twenty-five seconds."

I acknowledged his curiosity with a nod. Ted took another sip and said, "You know, some billionaire financier should take over the damn gun companies. Fire management. Change the way they do business."

"Would take a lot of money and a lot of risk." I changed the subject. "I wish you'd have your first drink at dinner rather than lunch."

"I make it to work every morning."

"What about Mary? What about Jack?"

"What about him?"

"When he recovers, he's going to need special care. You'll need to be sober."

Mary shook her head in dismay and told Ted, "You may be the one needing care."

"I'll get clear when Jack pulls out of it." He yawned, and Mary gave us a look of frustration. He excused himself and went off to his bedroom. His departure lifted the tension.

Knowing Kelly wanted to keep Mary company, I decided to visit Jack alone. "I'm going to the hospital." As I left, curiosity guided me through the garage to check the recyclable bin. I was right: empty bottles of Seagram's gin sat at various angles atop a pile of other empties. My son would light up with big ideas when he was drunk, like buying up the firearm manufacturers. We had talked about how Hartford is the historic heart of America's firearm industry. He knew that several chief executives of nearby gun companies were members of the country club and were in my foursome a few times. Still, there may have been something in his idea. In my Wall Street career watching the economy and picking stocks, I'd studied correlations, like how job growth correlates to higher inflation or when a company hikes its quarterly dividend that correlates to a higher stock price. There was an undeniable correlation between the abundant manufacturing of assault rifles in the Connecticut River Valley—what I'd heard people call The Silicon Valley of firearms—and one of them getting into the hands of a local madman.

Jack had a private room in intensive care. After the shooting, he was rushed to the emergency room by ambulance. He was placed in a medically-induced coma to rest the body and calm the brain to allow him to heal. We waited in the ER overnight, and in the morning, Dr. Bertrand came to us to deliver test results: the internal bleeding in Jack's skull had stopped, but his brain was still inflamed. To reassure us he said, "There's a good expectation he will come out of this. But we don't know when." Now, as I stood at Jack's bedside, he lay motionless. His eyes were closed and his chest gently rose and fell; a breathing tube ran to his mouth from a machine and lines ran from his arms to fluid bags hanging on a silver pole. Monitors astride his bed beeped his vital signs.

Dr. Bertrand came in. I wanted to hear from him something more than assurances that Jack would come out of it. I needed something more than hope and expectation, words he had used before. I felt impatient, and he was an easy target. "I want the best experts to help my grandson. Bring them in from Europe. Bring them in from anywhere. I don't care how much it costs."

He winced. Despite my rude tone, he remained calm. "The doctors here are among the best in the country. In fact, staff here is frequently called for its perspective on difficult cases."

I softened my tone. "I'm sorry. I see. Okay. We'll be patient." Maybe I needed another pill.

He left, and I took Jack's hand. I felt for the gold pinky ring Kelly and I had given him for his birthday, but it wasn't there. I rubbed the indentation the ring made on his skin, thinking that if he could feel the irritation, he might react with a twitch or show any kind of movement. But he didn't. I placed his hand back on the sheet. I pulled a chair up to the bed and opened the newspaper I had brought with me. When Jack was younger and we ate breakfast together on Saturdays, I read the famous comic strip *Zits* by the team of Scott and Borgman to him. I went slow because he often laughed uncontrollably. I bent down and whispered into his ear: "Hey Jack, let's see what Jeremy is up to today. Try not to laugh too hard. That might excite the nurses." I found the page. "Jeremy tells his dad, 'I'm anchoring the morning announcement this week. It kind of makes me a celebrity around school.'" I pointed my thumb to my big-shot self, mugged a smile, and glanced at Jack. There was no reaction. "Jeremy says, 'I hope I don't become difficult to live with.'" I frowned, as Jeremy's dad did in the comic strip, and deepened my voice to a lower pitch. "'You? Difficult? Never!'"

I had to stop. I blinked to clear my eyes; teardrops had formed dime-sized gray spots on the newsprint. I breathed a deep, cleansing breath. I folded the paper and gripped it with both hands. I mumbled to my grandson, "Jack, we'll wait for you till hell freezes over."

I earned tens of millions of dollars every year. Kelly and I were worth $1.1 billion. We owned a 125-foot custom-built yacht, a majority stake in the country club, timberland in Maine, and big investments in downtown Hartford office buildings. I was proud of my extensive portfolio of stocks, bonds, and other securities. I'd been profiled in the *New York Times* and appeared as a talking head on CNBC television to offer my analysis of the markets. I knew influential people and could get nearly anyone short of the president on the phone. Kelly and I had entertained the governor at our home and on our yacht, and I was close with the congressman who represented our district. I had enough cash to cover the cost of security guards at every school in Todd's Chapel for a century. Yet as I stood next to Jack, I couldn't dodge the irrefutable fact that everything I had, all my money and recognition, didn't amount to a damn thing.

"I'll see you tomorrow," I said before stepping out into the hallway. Across from Jack's room, a nurse stood at the door and gestured to the bed inside, quietly speaking to an attendant with a gurney, "We need to get this body down to the morgue." That drove home Jack's perilous condition

I needed a cup of coffee and drove to the diner. Traffic was light. I turned down Flowers Street. One of Ted's classmates who had lived here died a few years ago of opioid abuse. Next to the dead man's house was the home of one of Jack's wrestling teammates. Traffic cones stood at the front of the driveway to warn reporters not to bother the family. Police caution tape ran between the cones like a yellow ribbon of sorrow. Twin killers, drugs and guns, resided on Flowers Street.

The diner was nearly empty. A customer who arrived just ahead of me sat at the counter. The waitress placed a menu before him; their greetings to one another sounded inert. I took a seat near him and ordered coffee. CNN was on several televisions hung from the stainless steel walls, so it was impossible not to hear the news anchor glibly call the carnage in Todd's Chapel the "wrestling match massacre." He was hosting a panel discussion on gun violence. A panelist said: "We've accepted these events as routine." A second panelist who had lost a daughter at Virginia Tech demanded closure: "I want gun company executives to be called before Congress and be forced to tell the American people why they sell military rifles to civilians. I want them to be held accountable for choosing profits over children's lives."

That panelist had a definite goal, an admirable one to inspire a personal crusade. I had never felt passionately for or against reforming our gun laws. I knew very little about guns. When I was young, I'd heard shots fired from apartment building rooftops in Hartford celebrating the Fourth of July. During race riots in the late 1960s, I heard gunfire uptown, and news reports of the rioters killed didn't mean much to me, a kid in high school. I never lived in a violent neighborhood where Black mothers despaired street shootings involving their sons. There were no bad neighborhoods in Todd's Chapel.

I drank my coffee and paid at the cashier. The woman there knew me; we often exchanged friendly banter about her job, her customers, or anything just to be sociable. She thanked me by name but that was it. Her eyes flickered briefly, and she looked down at the bill. The nature of her job gave her the most rudimentary connection with anyone who stepped before her, a chance to share a good word. But this time, she averted her eyes as she gave me my change. I think she feared saying the wrong thing.

I went outside and overheard two men finishing their lunchtime conversation. One said, "Guns are just a tool if used properly." The other said in a cynical tone, "That's a big 'if.' It just seems there's nothing to be done about them." I watched them separate, get into their cars and drive away, still hearing the echo of "nothing to be done." Were we truly helpless? I wondered. I went to my car but did not get in. It was quiet. I stood perfectly still and listened hard, as if a moment of complete silence could help me comprehend the context of what had happened to Todd's Chapel. There was no traffic, no tolling of bells, not even the cold rush of winter wind through the trees. The stillness reminded me of TV commentary after some previous mass murder: "Grief and silence covered the town like a pestilential haze." I sensed this in my town, this stillness and pain like a pestilence.

I drove slowly through town. On the lawn outside Town Hall, homemade wooden crosses had quickly sprouted from a makeshift burial ground. I slowed nearly to a crawl. I was too far to identify the pictures affixed at the top of each crude cross, but I counted sixteen, one for each student killed in the gymnasium. Flanking the crosses were bouquets of flowers and lit candles. I pulled to the curb and watched a box truck drive around the town square. On its side the words "Duck and Cover" had been daubed in white. The truck kept circling. I knew about this truck; a news report several years ago said it had driven around the Capitol building in Washington after the slaughter at Marjory Stoneman Douglas High School in Parkland. It then traveled to the next massacre, and it was here now. The driver must be on the road constantly. He'd leave, the flowers on the makeshift graves would wilt, and the candles would flicker out, each ending its life naturally, as if symbolizing the end of the nation's attention to the siege of gun violence here. I've shared a drink with the executive editor of the *Hartford Courant* at the club, and I thought of calling her to suggest a story: "National mourning in Todd's Chapel to run out of oxygen."

As I headed home, I realized my awareness had shifted. When was the last time I'd looked this closely at my town? Decades ago when I started my career, I didn't think much about other people's problems. I reached home, turned past the gate and up the curving drive to my front door, and stopped beneath the portico. I shut off the engine and sat still for the better part of an hour. Back in 1981, I was absorbed in my job. I could still remember my first big profitable deal. It was a typical floor trader's swindle, but it ended well, and that was all I cared about. I worked on the stock exchange floor for a boutique wire house, an up-front view of buying and selling stocks. Humphrey, my boss, introduced me to a hedge fund manager who had stopped by our post. This fellow boasted about how quickly his fund's value was growing. But Humphrey was wise to this guy. When the fund manager moved on, Humphrey gave me the fund's stock symbol. "Keep an eye on these shares." When the 1982 bull market began in August, those shares jumped. Four months later, this fund manager falsely overstated his assets in a magazine article. Humphrey began shorting the shares, and I learned at his side. A week later he very offhandedly and by way of a third party flagged his observation of fraud to securities regulators. The boastful promoter got busted, the hedge fund's shares cratered, and I got $20,000 as a share in Humphrey's shrewd play. It was so dispassionate, so efficient.

I thought I'd cheer up if I went inside the house, but that didn't happen. Mitchell, our butler, took my coat and then brought me a glass of red wine as I settled into the living room. He told me Kelly was resting in our bedroom. I continued to dwell on my life of making money. I had put in long hours, paid attention, and followed the herd of investors. I made good money for my clients and myself. After twenty years working for Wall Street investment houses, my colleague at Goldman Sachs, Andrew Pritchard, suggested we start our own hedge fund. Boy, was Andy driven. He was also brilliant; I went along with him, and we did very well.

But looking back now at one decision we made, my better judgment failed me: We invested in the stocks of the gun manufacturing industry. I'd spent a lifetime on Wall Street believing the choices I made didn't hurt anyone. Now I saw that wasn't true.

Mitchell refilled my wine glass. The light of afternoon on the picture window became the softer light of dusk. Mila, our maid, placed dinner prepared by our chef on the table. Kelly joined me for an unusually quiet meal. She tried to start a conversation. She asked me about Jack. She asked where else I had been. I gave her short answers. Finally, she said, "I've rarely seen you so pensive."

I stared at my plate for a few seconds recalling a story I heard from a Jesuit professor in college about the guilt St. Augustine felt after he stole from an orchard. This pried open my own feelings of guilt. I faced Kelly squarely and shook my head. "It's funny how you can reasonably excuse all of your previous behavior. When I was growing up, everyone thought I was a smart, pious boy. As an altar boy, the priests and nuns liked me. They encouraged me. Yet after serving at Sunday Mass, I jumped the fence to steal pears from Mrs. Downing's yard. God would understand. I had just worked for him. These pears were like gold. But Mrs. Downing had been watching, and one Sunday, she caught me. From her door, she leveled a finger at me and shouted. 'Emil, are you snitching my pears again?' I felt I had to atone. For the next several years, I carried her packages home from Dad's store. Years later, I was no better. My girlfriend and I spent Saturday evenings at a motel. I stupidly left a receipt in my dad's car. When he and mom found out, they were upset, less about the sex and more about my lies. I did a lot of walking after that incident."

"I'm glad you didn't run off with her." Kelly smiled to reassure me. "All of that sounds so innocent."

I made a fist and placed my thumb to my lower lip. "At work, I took advantage of situations on the exchange floor to scalp a thousand here, a thousand there, making the seed money for the wealth we enjoy today. My actions were unethical, maybe even illegal, but I saw it as acceptable Mob behavior among floor traders. Later on, when I made money for wealthy clients, they looked at me approvingly. They would not have cared one fig if I told them the elaborate corners I sometimes cut to earn it." I shifted in the chair. "I never had any nagging concerns about all this."

Her expression changed from apt listener to concern for me. "This isn't about Jack or Ted. What is it?"

I came out with it. "I made more than $25 million investing in gun stocks. Buying these shares pushed up the market value of the gun companies. That gave them the cash to hire the best lobbyists in Washington. The NRA's influence became colossal, and now guns are everywhere. I've been going over this for several hours now, and I can't get past how this thoughtlessness helped perpetuate gun violence."

"You never told me this."

I took a deep breath, and my chest shuddered. "When Andy Pritchard first suggested in 2004 that we invest in the gun industry, I said, 'Guns have a social cost.' But he silenced my mere squeak of a complaint by explaining why the timing was right. When the ban on sales of assault weapons expired that year, we bought these stocks hand over fist. The next year, Washington passed the law that shields manufacturers from liability when a gun is used in a crime. A few years later, the Supreme Court placed few limits on the private ownership of guns. That was good for the sales of pistols and rifles. Private equity firms rolled up smaller gun companies into conglomerates, reducing competition. Share prices rose. Hundreds of big money investors saw this opportunity, too. We all made millions."

I remembered more details. "After Sandy Hook, people who owned guns got scared the government would approve tighter restrictions on guns. That accelerated sales, and profits rose." I paused to stress what came next. "When we cashed in our investments, we made $50 million. That money was commingled with our other assets. Who knew? My $25 million split was anonymous profit then. But it's haunting me now."

Kelly folded her dinner napkin. "What did Andy say to persuade you?"

"That making money was not a liberal or conservative political act. He only judged his actions by their outcome, wealth creation, rather than by any obligation to consider what it means if everyone did the same thing. The shooting here, our son's drinking, the dreariness of downtown mocks our arrogant assumption that our wealth keeps us safe. It's not true. Everyone's life hangs by a thread."

We moved to the sofa, where Mitchell served us cordials. We sat quietly, allowing my confession to settle in. A vehicle's lights flashed across the window and we heard a car arrive at the portico. Mitchell let Father Rushmore in, and it was clear the priest had a stressful day. His face was swollen red like he had been wiping away tears.

"You look like you need a drink."

Rushmore sat down on the sofa across from us. We'd become close friends as parishioners at Blessed Sacrament. "That's one thing I came for, a drink," he said. To Mitchell, he said, "Make it a tall Scotch and soda." He shifted in his seat several times trying to get comfortable.

"I was over at the hospital and heard Jack was the same. I'm heartsick over him. He's in my prayers," he began. I nodded thanks. "It took several days, but Rabbi Noah, Reverend Dyson, and I have been to every house that lost someone. Of the twenty dead, sixteen are children. The death toll will rise; a suicide by a father grieving for his daughter, a sibling's drug overdose. Witnessing spectacular violence ruins many lives of those left behind, and given how close-knit this town is, we're all witnesses." He accepted a glass from Mitchell and drank lustily. With his free hand, he covered his eyes and pulled his hand down hard on his face as if to wipe away the strain. He exhaled audibly and gestured to Mitchell for a top-off.

"Is there something we can do?" I said.

"That's the second reason I'm here, to ask a favor. Governor Alston will be at tomorrow's funeral Mass. Will you serve as an usher?"

The day had been long and exhausting. I didn't want to repeat it. But before I could answer, he went on: "The world is watching us. You've seen the reporters from across the country converging here. Today at Starbucks they stepped in the way of people coming out with their coffee to ask questions. They know the governor will be at Mass. The town needs to show that it's holding itself together, and we need our notable citizens to be visible to show we're not just victims with funeral processions and yellow police tape." He drank again and looked away as he said, "I selfishly thought earlier today that if only a severe hurricane in Florida would cut short the news coverage here. But it's the wrong season."

"Is the governor planning a news conference?"

"He'll spend a moment at the lectern." Before I could speak, he went on, "Emil, this town has two institutions—and you're one of them. I seem to be the other one, in some small way. Everyone comes to me as a sounding board for their troubles. But you're the franchise. Everyone knows what you and Kelly have done. You didn't want the Scordato family name on the new oncology wing in Hartford, but the millions you gave were noted in the newspapers. You funded the town's new sports complex. Others have your public spirit. But you'll be noticed."

"Okay. Just tell me what time."

The priest nodded his thanks, leaned over to the coffee table, and set down his empty glass. "Mass starts at ten. Be there at nine. Also, Congressman Bixby is up from Washington. He'll be there too."

2

THE CHURCH WAS PACKED AGAIN, this time for a murdered wrestler, a senior. I greeted Governor Malcolm Alston and his wife, Theresa, and led them up front. When the Mass began, I stood in the back but had a hard time following along. I was hounded again by thoughts of personal misgivings. Years ago, when I was occasionally staying overnight in the city, I had an affair with a young woman, a colleague. Kelly found out and it nearly ruined our marriage. I was shaken and needed advice; I got it from an elderly fellow at the club. We were dressing in the men's locker room when he told me that if a personal catastrophe happened that was outside of my control, feel the regret and fix the damage as best I could. If the catastrophe was self-inflicted, feel the guilt and shame. Perform some kind of penance, and move on. Kelly and I worked to resolve our problem. I told her it would never happen again, but that wasn't enough. She extracted a promise to renew our vows, which we did. That fling was another regrettable instance of poor judgment.

The governor stood to speak, and I refocused on the Mass. His words were a call for everyone to stand together. "Evil has a way of ad-libbing its way into our lives. But we can't let sadness and suspicion keep us from gathering with one another, socializing, and visiting our places of worship. The nation's unity is woven with roads from one small town to another, including those grieving after gun violence. Todd's Chapel is one of these towns. Don't allow fear to make this a ghost town."

Mass ended and people filed out. I stood at the top of the steps. Congressman Bixby joined me. He'd just begun his tenth term representing the district that included Todd's Chapel. I helped finance his campaign, just as I had the career of his father, former Representative Clement Bixby.

Bixby was from a long line of New England Brahmins. After arriving from England in 1830, they rose from farmers to judges to respected holders of elective office. Sam Bixby was an excellent listener when mingling with constituents at farmers' markets, and when Boy Scout troops recognized new Eagle Scouts. Like his father, he held moderate Democratic views, but he differed in one crucial way: the elder Bixby's speeches to the House were a deadpan, low-voiced monotone that put listeners to sleep. When Sam debated in the chamber, he spoke with a rousing fluency that bellowed to the rafters. Elected officials in Connecticut after Sandy Hook had placed gun safety as a top legislative priority. So did Sam Bixby. The political media in Washington saw him as a leading voice on the issue. I wondered whether he would use today's funeral as another platform.

The governor stood at his limousine door, offering reporters a final comment. When he ducked inside, they rushed up to Bixby. One reporter asked about the bill he co-sponsored to repeal the federal law shielding the gun industry from victim lawsuits. Bixby waited for this question to trail off and answered it with a question of his own.

"What's the difference between a cyanide pill and an assault rifle?" The reporter blinked. The others moved in. Bixby said, "You can't get your hands on a cyanide pill." He waited for them to scribble down his words. "You all know insurers paid the $73 million Sandy Hook settlement. My bill strips gun makers of the federal liability shield. When it becomes law, the nation's insurance industry will take center stage in solving our gun violence crisis. It will force gunsmiths to reduce their risks of doing business. Washington's dysfunction will be a sideshow."

Another reporter asked, "Will the tragedy here help your bill?"

"I only need two or three votes."

The reporters moved on, and I returned to Bixby's side. "You didn't really answer that last question."

"That's because what happened in Todd's Chapel won't matter a damned bit in Washington. My conservative colleagues promised a pitched battle against my bill. I'm not sure how to outflank them."

"I should know more about all this."

"Spend time in Washington. People have heard of you. Just seeing you would be like flashing your wallet. You might get me those votes."

3

I CONSIDERED WHETHER it was fair to leave my family for a few days in Washington during our troubles, but Bixby's invitation was a chance to satisfy an itch I felt to try to do something about guns. His staff called to say it had lined up meetings with House conservatives. I agreed to go, but before I could, I had to attend to a family financial matter Kelly had insisted we needed to do.

When we made our first $500 million, we hired an attorney to write up an inheritance and distribution plan that included trusts for Ted and his family. Within seven years, my portfolio had doubled to $1.1 billion, and it was that additional $600 million Kelly wanted given away in a tax-efficient, methodical way. She convinced me to talk to a professional.

"You're seventy. If you die or something catches us by surprise, I don't want the IRS hounding me for taxes because we didn't plan thoroughly."

Kelly was the oldest of four children in an Irish Catholic family from Kew Gardens, Queens. When her father, a New York police officer, lost his job because of his heavy drinking, she increased her college course load to graduate six months early. She moved home and took a job teaching fifth grade at a nearby Catholic school. The school didn't pay well, but the job helped the family cover its bills and still gave her time to attend a stock broker training program at Merrill Lynch. I was one of the presenters. I recognized her intelligence and the proud way she carried her tall, slender frame, and when we spoke, her smile seemed so genuine. We dated, and after four months, she moved into my Upper East Side apartment. Living with me allowed her to help her parents even more.

Years later, when Ted and Carol were in grammar school and I was earning upward of $5 million a year in income alone, we moved into a fifteen-room home in Todd's Chapel. It was here that Kelly slipped comfortably into the role of the glamorous woman of the house. At first, she hosted cocktail parties for charitable events, but then we began holding dinner parties for political candidates, their spouses, and a few neighbors. One night, we were getting ready in our bedroom. She sat at her mirror combing her hair. Mitchell had brought up a bottle of champagne. I opened it with a theatrical pop, filled two glasses, and gave one to her. I stood behind her, and she looked up at my reflection.

I told her, "Our butler is downstairs greeting important people at our front door. Our chef has been preparing hors d'oeuvre for days, and our maid has flowers everywhere. My wife is becoming more beautiful by the second." She flicked her eyebrows playfully while not taking her gaze from the fine work of powdering her cheeks. I went on, "I couldn't be more pleased." I raised my glass. "To us!"

To get on with our updated philanthropic planning, I set up an appointment with Tyler Buchanan, who ran an advisory fund that systematically sent donations from high-net-worth individuals to charities and worthy causes around the world. We met for lunch in Stamford. I told him, "Our charitable giving has been hit and run. Fifty million for an oncology wing in honor of my dad who died of cancer. Landmark gifts to Manhattanville where Kelly got her degree and to Boston College where I got my Bachelor's. A million every year to the archdiocese. We just gave five million to a victims' fund in my town."

Tyler said, "Sad scenes worthy of funding are everywhere. Several of my clients are helping Ukraine rebuild. Another is improving irrigation in Africa. Now this is an essential question: Do you want to give everything away in your lifetime and watch where it goes?"

"That wouldn't be easy. Our assets grow so fast, they get ahead of us."

"You're not alone. The financial markets have minted a breed of enormously wealthy individuals I call the non-noteworthy billionaire."

"Non-noteworthy billionaire?"

"Investors who rode the stock market to a net worth of a billion dollars even though they hadn't distinguished themselves in their careers or in society in any way. Now they don't have a clue. Then there's someone like Red Ettinger. He built a business worth $5 billion and gave it all away during his lifetime. He donated to health clinics in poor parts of Africa and to public education in Alabama, Arkansas, and Louisiana. When he was down to a few million that he and his wife could live on, he sold his house and they moved into an apartment. Done. Finished. No longer a billionaire."

I thought of the lifestyle Kelly had come to enjoy. "I'm not sure my wife could settle for apartment living. We could sell the house in Todd's Chapel and live on our yacht."

He smiled. "That wouldn't impress Red Ettinger. He'd want you to sell the yacht and take up residence in a houseboat on the Housatonic."

He asked about my family background. I'd never been hesitant to tell people my father owned a pork store on Franklin Avenue in Hartford's Italian neighborhood and that we lived upstairs. I began by saying dad had fought in Europe during the war and my grandfather had arrived penniless from Sicily in 1919. "They set me up to have a good life."

"They'd be proud to know you're the family's first philanthropist."

Strictly speaking, that wasn't true, though I hesitated to correct Tyler. My paternal grandfather, Pietro, had a reputation for public generosity, but his story had a dark side that I kept secret. Somehow I trusted Tyler with this colorful part of the family story, so I told him.

"During the Depression, my grandfather helped struggling

neighbors," I began. Tyler put down his fork to listen closely. "He was a typical early twentieth-century Sicilian immigrant who worked with his hands, but he wanted more. His wife, my grandmother Concetta, told me bits and pieces of his life, usually when she came to breakfast on Saturdays. I'd hear her climbing the stairs; she'd be carrying a tall brown paper bag with Italian loaves sticking out. By then I had sectioned a half grapefruit and set it at her usual place. She sat and told stories. When I headed downstairs to work in Dad's store, she handed me a quarter from her black pocketbook and said, 'Light a votive candle for your grandfather.'"

Tyler's face lit up. I went on: "One Christmas Eve during the Depression, he went shopping on Front Street, the original Little Italy in Hartford. It was late, and a street vendor still had unsold Christmas trees. He gave the man money. When my grandfather arrived home, he told my father, 'Carmen, go to the families who live two and three to an apartment, and if they need a tree, tell them the corner vendor has one for them. Tell them to use my name.' The day after Christmas, the vendor came around for full payment, as my grandfather had arranged."

"He must have become successful."

"He worked for a funeral home. He dug graves at first but later drove a hearse with a team of horses. He also built coffins." I paused. I had never told anyone what I was about to say. "Once when Grandma repeated the Christmas Eve story, she added with an edge of remorse, 'He didn't like being poor. He was on the streets night and day. But he was no bone-breaker.' I was eleven or twelve, too young to interpret her emotions but still curious, so I asked my father, 'What did Grandma mean?' But he dismissed my question. A while later, I asked my Uncle Leo, his brother. Leo gave me the details. Turns out Pietro did jobs for the Mob. The coffins he built had a secret lower compartment for the gangsters to stash away the bodies of their victims. For this, he was well paid. He must have liked the extra illegal money because he and two friends pulled off a few jobs of their own. Two months after the episode of Christmas Eve generosity, he was gunned down. Uncle Leo learned later that a rival gang was upset that Pietro and his friends had hijacked a truck bringing Christmas trees in from Vermont. The trio had sold the trees to a middleman, who distributed them to the street vendors."

"He knew about the extra trees?"

"My uncle deduced Pietro and his associates made the fatal mistake of not pistol-whipping the drivers into silence. One identified the hijackers to a member of the Mob, and soon all three were dead. Not roughing up the drivers was my grandmother's appraisal of her husband's gentle hand, though it led to his murder."

"Incredible story," Tyler said. His advice for our next phase of philanthropy was simple: Kelly and I had to compile a list of social needs we were passionate about. "Think about dire situations around the world but also small needs nearby. You could pay for new inner-city playgrounds or schools, or summer camps for worthy poor kids. Could be one-time grants or annual donations. We'll update the list every November. Add a name and I'll begin making distributions in January."

"I'll ask my wife for input." Kelly had often repeated her mother's rule that charity began at home.

"What about you? What motivates you most?"

"I've been thinking lately about solutions to gun violence."

"If you did something about that you'd be in the company of Michael Bloomberg, Oprah Winfrey, and Bennett Durso," he said. He thought for a second and added, "Yet despite the millions they've given, the problem hasn't improved. Keep me posted."

I was eager to come up with Tyler's list. Being a philanthropist was a far cry from my relationship with money when I was young. As I got older, the farther away from home I went, around Hartford at first and then to Boston for college, I felt constrained by my empty pockets. Plainly speaking, I was cheap. I stiffed a few bartenders with something less than flat-rate tips. After college, I had to work; I didn't have the option of becoming a back-to-the-earth rucksack wanderer in the 1970s for a few years like some classmates. As my wealth grew over the years, I never felt money was filthy lucre or had a visceral feeling of avarice. I put in the long hours to earn it, and when I had a good deal of it, I enjoyed lavishing it on Kelly and our kids. I helped my parents retire comfortably by buying them a home in Pompano Beach. Over time, I understood that I could become very generous to people and situations beyond the family. I donated quietly, often anonymously, and rarely conspicuously. That changed when a photograph of Kelly and me handing a mocked-up, oversized check for $50 million to a hospital executive made the newspapers. Since then, I enjoyed hand-delivering a donation check here and there. Kelly now accused me of over-compensating for my skinflint years. That may have been true. I felt for those who struggled for a fair chance at a good life.

During the Occupy Wall Street demonstrations in 2011, I called Liberato's Pizza near Zuccotti Park and sent twenty-five pies over, though I kept it a secret; my country club buddies would have considered me a traitor. Every year, I gave $1 million to Father Rushmore at Christmas to help him meet the archbishop's expectation that he reverse the steady decline in parish revenues. Believe me, it feels a lot better to be generous than cheap.

4

I FLEW TO WASHINGTON by private jet and checked into the Phoenix Hotel across from Union Station, an easy walk across the Capitol to the Rayburn building. Sam Bixby's chief of staff had arranged meetings with House members from districts where a mass killing had occurred, with the idea that these members might have an open mind about his gun safety legislation if a respectable third party appealed to them. I was the third party. A commitment to donate the legal maximum to them directly, their party coffers, and their political action committees might seal the deal. But only three congressmen agreed to meet me, two at their Rayburn offices and one, Clayton Jeffries, over cocktails that evening at his longtime family home in Georgetown.

"You'll enjoy Jeffries," Bixby said. "We're something of sparring partners since we entered the House the same year. He's from Virginia and is a board member at the NRA. He speaks quite knowingly about gun rights. I went with him and his wife to Dover when their only son's body was brought home from Iraq. He's been devastated ever since about losing him to war."

One session was with Barney Bumgarner, a long-serving congressman from Texas. "He's a crusty 80-year-old Army veteran. I think he wants to meet you out of curiosity. Not too many billionaires in his district," Bixby said. "You'll also stop in and see Clyde Sutter first. A thoughtful guy." He came around his desk to see me to the door. "Emil, you're a lobbyist now. You'll see what it's like to walk the halls of Congress frustrated that although you wave around a checkbook, you can't always buy influence. Try to have some fun while getting pissed off. "

I stopped in to see Sutter first. He was elected in November to his fourth term in a district where six people had been killed at the Kansas State Fair. I took a seat in his staff office and waited. What had Bixby said, that I'm a lobbyist now, an advocate for a cause? Never expected to be in this position. I reminded myself to smile. I looked at the portraits hanging on the wall and the faces all looked serious. They couldn't have been lobbyists. Sutter came out to greet me. He shook my hand and invited me into his office.

"Bixby's staff said your grandson is in a coma from the Todd's Chapel shooting. I hope he makes it." He sounded sincere. He was about forty, with thin sandy hair, and had a genial way about him. He first served in Congress in his early thirties, so although he was still young, he was a seasoned politician.

I said, "I understand you're from the Columbine generation. Attended high school in Oakley, not all that far from the Colorado border."

"That's right. I've visited Columbine High School in Littleton. I've also been to Aurora to see the movie house where the midnight rampage took place."

"Right, the massacre in a theater by the guy dressed in full battle gear. Awful. Listen, I know you're a busy man, so I'll get straight to it. You've gone back and forth on gun safety. Before the killing at the state fair, you backed gun rights. But afterward, you said there's no reason a civilian should own a gun designed for the battlefield. Changing your priorities because gun violence has touched your community is a powerful argument. People will commend you for it. Support Bixby's bill. Nothing in it confiscates guns or denies rightful ownership. Break from party orthodoxy, and I'll donate to you and your PAC as much as the law allows every year you're in office."

"I appreciate your offer." Sutter tapped the end of a pen on his desk blotter as if counting off a few seconds. He chose his words carefully. "My district in western Kansas is rural. Rural folks are more knowledgeable than many people think. They know I have an A rating from the NRA because I've affirmed gun rights. If I vote for that bill, no matter how watered-down Republicans make it, I'll lose that rating. I might as well write my own political death warrant. My voters will elect whomever the NRA endorses, and it will no longer be me. The bill's going to be defeated anyway. So why sacrifice myself?"

His words were open and honest, but his body language told me that he wasn't all that comfortable with the forces that restrained him. I had to appeal to him in blunt terms. "I've done that, too, placing my personal interests over doing the right thing. Sometimes on Wall Street, making big money is all that matters. In your business, it's votes. But Congressman, here's your chance to make a wide impact. I will give the legal max, from here on down the line."

"You're free to do that. I can't say it will sway my vote." The session ended with his thoughtful words: "I hope your grandson makes a full recovery."

I thanked him for his time and concern and went down the hall to see Barney Bumgarner, who immediately dismissed my courtesy when I said I appreciated him giving me time.

"Bixby trots you in here to talk to me when he should have paid an Uber to take you around the back country of Texas. My country." He stroked his white goatee and inspected me. "If you knew our culture, our etiquette, you'd think differently about owning a gun. We pack 'em, and everybody feels safe. For those who hunt, it's the cheapest way to keep your belly full."

He also knew that Jack was in the hospital. I told him, "My interest in this bill comes from standing next to my grandson's bedside after a terrible random shooting. That and the twenty people murdered."

"Did the police get that gunman?"

"Yes sir, they did."

"The score is settled, then."

"I wouldn't say twenty to one is an even score. What about the next shooting and the one after that? There's been an ongoing series of massacres in Texas, even one in your district."

"There are remedies that aren't being used. Laws that exist that aren't enforced—like mental health screenings. We should arm every teacher."

"Why not help Bixby improve those laws? Force gunsmiths to market guns thoughtfully rather than promote assault weapons as a way to demonstrate one's manhood."

Bumgarner ceased fingering his beard and pointed at me. "You think too much of what's possible. America is overrated. It's too violent, too racist, too greedy. People are unreliable. But guns! Now guns are reliable. Owning a gun gives supporters of gun rights something that people fighting for abortion rights and transgender equality don't have. We have militias in every state. We're past the tipping point for taking away our guns. I will tell you, if pushed too far, we can mount an insurrection. Try it, and the federal government will become irrelevant. You ever thought of that?"

I shook my head in disbelief. "That can't happen."

"No? Texans don't think like you. Listen here. I thought you might be a square fellow with a fair offer of support. But we don't need your big Eastern money." He dipped his chin to his neck, deepened his voice to accentuate its grave tone, pointed to the door, and tried to belittle me: "Young man, my aide will show you out."

I better understood what Bixby meant about lobbyists: they needed a double-thick hide. I was glad other congressmen declined to meet me and that I didn't walk the halls knocking on doors that would be slammed in my face.

Later that afternoon, I met up with Bixby to ride out to Georgetown to Clayton Jeffries's home. In the car, Bixby went over Jeffries's Southern background, how he'd achieved his father's hopes that he would one day serve in public office. Jeffries's family made its fortune in Virginia tobacco over a century ago, but his elders preferred to exert political influence from behind the scenes. His grandfather purchased an interest in a minor league baseball team in Lynchburg in the thirties and full ownership of a Richmond radio station. Candidates he supported plied the ballpark's box seats and bleachers with a smile. They extolled conservative interests on the radio. Their election helped Republicans during the Depression to break the long Democratic dominance in the state. The next in line was Jeffries's father, Clayton II. He wanted his only son to extend the family's reach to moneyed interests in New York and Boston by attending an Ivy League school. In many ways, the man I was to meet was like the Jeffries men before him: a gregarious patrician with an educated Virginian drawl. But during the seventies he was less a student of politics and money and more a wealthy young man with a wide circle of drinking and concert-going friends. He got into the University of Virginia in '76 only through family influence. Bixby summed up his gentleman's charm: "Clayton's talk is like horse shit. It comes out smooth but doesn't hang together. After a while, you get to the heart of things and he can be reasonable. I enjoy his company."

The late afternoon rays of the February sun were dimming over the unbroken line of stone and brick houses on O Street when we arrived at the one that had been in Jeffries's family for generations. We got out, stepped over ancient silvery trolley tracks embedded in smooth cobblestones and slid between parked foreign cars. A leaping silver Jaguar on the hood of one car and a shiny three-pointed star on another car shimmered in lamplight, prompting memories of the hood ornaments I stole for my collection when I was a street kid in Hartford.

Jeffries had a knack for inviting friends and rivals in Congress over for drinks to keep the Capitol Hill conversation going. Bixby and I were running late. As we approached the door, a glimpse through a window revealed a glowing fireplace, its light glinting from cocktail glasses in the hands of two men in conversation. Bixby knocked, and we were welcomed by Sara Jeffries, the congressman's wife.

"My apologies, Sara. A late meeting with staff. May I introduce Emil Scordato, a friend from home."

Sara smiled broadly. Her eyes lit up, "Sam, you just missed it. Clayton told the story about Senator Billings's aide who intentionally spilled coffee on the *Post* reporter who described Billings as a skinflint."

"I read the story," he said, and quickly relayed the details to me. "Billings conveniently goes off to the men's room when a restaurant bill arrives at the table. Yet he awkwardly stooped to pick up a silver coin from a sidewalk. The *Post* story hit that octogenarian in the eye. Maybe now he'll retire."

As I'd glimpsed, a fireplace was ablaze in the den. Jeffries hailed our arrival and gestured toward the bar. "Sam, good to see you." He looked over at me. "Emil, nice to finally meet you." He poured both of us a bourbon on the rocks. "We've been stuck talking about how to reform the presidential primary schedule. But now that you're both here, we'll pivot to guns."

The other guest, Lionel Sager, came over and nodded greetings to Bixby. Jeffries introduced me. Sager was a liberal Democratic congressman from Maryland in his second term. We formed a loose circle standing and raised our glasses to one another.

Jeffries directed his first question to me, "Did you enjoy your day on Capitol Hill?"

"Time well spent, especially with Congressman Bumgarner. He told me that guns were like a reliable pet at your side and threatened me with an armed insurrection. Then he booted me out of his office." This amused everyone. "To him, the gun safety issue is tantamount to war."

"He kicks up dust like a mule," Jeffries said. "But I like the way he votes."

Sager said, "I hope he helps solve our other problems. Today it's social media's spread of harmful content. Last week it was military funding to keep pace with China. As for guns, we've become inured to the problem. Massacres in America have become like Peruvian bus plunges; unless twenty-five people die, a bus disaster in the Andes is not reported around the world because the world has ceased to care. God help us."

Jeffries said, "Republicans agree gun violence is a problem. Few will say it's a big problem. You solve it with police presence and by prohibiting the mentally unfit from getting their hands on guns. I'm for universal background checks, five-day waiting periods at dealers and gun shows, banning ghost guns, and a favorite of mine, making sure guns are locked securely at home. I've received pushback from my side of the aisle when saying that. I can take it. But hear this: I'm against any restrictions on hardware available to the law-abiding citizen."

"What about Sam's bill?" asked Sager.

Jeffries looked at Bixby and said back to Sager. "I'm against it. Canceling the federal liability shield gives the insurance industry too much power. Without that shield, no insurance executive in his right mind will sell a gun manufacturing outfit a liability policy." Then he turned to me. "You're from Hartford. The insurers there won't go bankrupt for the sake of their longtime gun-making clients in Connecticut. Emil, you're a professional money manager. Am I right?"

"Yes, but it seems— "

He cut me off. "Without insurance, you have no industry. We'd have to create a new federal insurance program like we did in the 1950s for the nuclear energy industry when it was thought to be too dangerous to calculate the investment risks. Back then, the big Hartford carriers wanted no part of it. But nuclear held promise, so Washington devised a federal backstop. If Sam's bill becomes law, a similar plan for gunsmiths will be essential."

As I watched him in conversation, it appeared that one of Jeffries's virtues was an absence of vanity. He didn't let the cigar ash that speckled his suit jacket interrupt him from pressing his argument. He worked hunter's idioms into his banter; Bixby was "barking up the wrong tree" with this bill. He poured himself another glass of bourbon, and the booze didn't light up anger in his voice; if anything, he became more genial. I wondered if Bixby could bring him over to his side. Could Jeffries break free from his party dogma?

Sager said, "If Washington devised a federal insurance program, Congress would want a degree of control over the gunsmiths."

Jeffries responded, "Exactly! That's the crux of the matter. The gun companies would be at the mercy of meddlers rather than the market." He looked to Bixby. "Nothing—not even if a red state senator's wife was shot dead at the Kennedy Center—will get this approved. I'm sorry, Sam, but your chances are slim to none."

We sat down to a simple meal of grilled fish with potatoes and vegetables; the butler served Virginia vintages of red and white wine. We talked about immigration. Sager knew a waiter named Sebastian at a popular Maryland restaurant who had grown up in Medellin, the Colombian city that for many years was controlled by the drug kingpin Pablo Escobar. Gang violence there had fractured daily life. Sebastian left when he was sixteen to follow his older brother to the Netherlands, where they both worked in the restaurant industry. "He told me he felt safe and secure there," Sager said. "He could leave his bicycle in one place at night and it would be there the next morning. Not so in Medellin." Sebastian fell in love with a young woman, they got married and planned to have a family. "His wife wanted their children to grow up in America, but Sebastian argued against it. He didn't want to lose his newfound sense of safety. Medellin was too profound a memory."

Sager astutely painted his story into a larger picture. "The tens of thousands arriving at our Southern border make the treacherous journey from places of violent conflict, poverty, and political repression. Some fear rising seas back home. They may or may not know of the gun violence here. Even if they do, it doesn't matter. They come to America eager to work and want their children to become Americans," he said. "But it's different with people in much of Europe. Violence here is a big disqualifier. News about America is everywhere overseas. Some Europeans—well, they think twice about emigrating here because of it. They don't even want to come for a vacation."

"But this young man changed his mind. Why did he move to Maryland?" Jeffries wanted to know.

"His older brother took a job as a chef in a two-star restaurant in Columbia. He persuaded Sebastian that the Columbia in Maryland was far safer than the Colombia of their youth. He overcame his reservations, and he and his wife came. They have a little boy."

Listening, I thought of how ironic it was that Europeans would consider their nations safer than the United States, since American soldiers had twice crossed the Atlantic to free them from the grip of war. But I couldn't deny the observation; owning a gun was so ingrained in American society from when frontiersmen and colonists carried a musket or flintlock pistol everywhere. Guns were still everywhere. But flintlocks were nothing compared to the power of assault weapons that kill so randomly and quickly. We had to get them out of circulation.

It was a fine evening, and when it was over, we thanked Jeffries and prepared to leave. As soon as our host's front door had closed behind us, Bixby said: "See what I mean? He's an interesting man. Full of shit, but earnest."

"Can you persuade him to change his vote?"

"I don't know. It's frustrating. I haven't been able to pick off the few votes I need. It's as if the opposition is taunting me to go outside the box." He sounded defeated.

On the Uber ride back, he said, "The only power left that might help are the markets. Any ideas?" I remembered that was what Ted had suggested.

"That wouldn't be easy," I told him. He looked interested, but before I could explain why, my phone buzzed. Kelly texted me to call, saying it was urgent. "I need to make a call," I said.

Bixby replied, "By all means."

When I reached Kelly, she said: "Ted was forced to close his dental office. He says it's for good. His assistant drove him home again." I told her I'd be home before noon the next day.

It had been four weeks since the shooting. Ted had become unreliable at work. He had begun drinking at his office and failed to keep his patient appointments. Today, he arrived home stinking of gin and announced to Mary that he wanted to sell his practice. I told Bixby all this and summed it up: "A dentist who breathes gin on people and whose hands shake can't see patients."

The first time we noticed Ted turn to the bottle was when he was twenty, up from Yale to say goodbye to his childhood dog Barkley. The dog was seventeen and could barely walk. We had just hired Mitchell to be our butler, and he witnessed everything. When the animal shelter attendant arrived, Ted handed his pet to the man, who carried it like a sleeping child to the rear of his van. He returned with Barkley's collar and gave it to Ted, whose eyes were filling with tears. After the van pulled away, he went to the bar in the den, pulled out a bottle of Scotch whisky, and downed two shots as quickly as he could pour them out. Mitchell didn't have the authority to scold our son. Ted took the bottle to the basement recreation room, and Mitchell could hear the television. Three hours later, Kelly found him bleary eyed and barely able to climb the stairs. Later that year, he came home from evenings out with his friends beastly drunk. He never complained about experiencing any kind of lovesickness, or any trauma. No matter how much Mitchell, at my insistence, boasted about the excellent wines we served at dinner, Ted preferred the hard stuff.

Kelly and I gave Ted everything. We shielded him from the most troublesome of college student worries: poor personal finances. When Jack was born, he seemed to curb his drinking. Kelly and I considered him the perfect co-host at our dinner parties and backyard socials, for Ted balanced social refinements with a drink in his hand. He made introductions politely and didn't force his opinions on others by raising his voice. He was never a nasty drunk. People liked Ted, and he liked people. He excelled in his career; his dentistry practice was always full. But by the end of every social event, he was usually ripped. Kelly and I were proud of our son. When we lost Carol, he understood we needed him more, and he gave us the attention. He dealt well with his own grief over losing his sister, often with a drink.

But after the massacre, Ted's stability cracked. He didn't care that he was a down-and-out drunk. He stocked a refrigerator at his office suite with gin and tonic. He took a belt between patients. His intoxication was obvious to his hygienist, and when his staff saw he was headed for a drunken afternoon, they canceled his appointments. He didn't put up a fight; that's what he wanted, time to be free to drink. By dinner, he had downed a fifth of gin and reached for beer. Afterward, he fell asleep watching television, and the next day was the same.

To say we were concerned was an understatement. Back from Washington, I went straight to Ted's house, where Kelly was waiting. Ted hadn't awakened yet. I asked, "When might he be back at work?"

"Not until he dries out," Kelly said. "He's sick. Dr. Bertrand will have to recommend a professional, though I wish we could just commit him."

My wife's eyes had lost all of their radiance, and I feared she was losing her resoluteness. I tried to comfort everyone. "I'll ask him to move back home. We'll get his best friends to speak to him."

"I wish to God Carol were here," Kelly said. "When she got knocked down at a soccer game, she got right back up. I don't understand why he isn't fighting like she did, for his own health and for his son." She began to weep. I tried to wrap my arms around her, but she pounded both fists against my chest before burying her head in it. "When we lost Carol, I thought nothing could be worse than losing a child at twenty. Now I'm losing my son and my grandson too."

Dr. Bertrand arrived, and we gave him an update. Mary said "Ted's dismissing all that he has in life. Nothing is any good, his career, who he is. If Jack dies, we're in deep trouble."

We heard Ted stirring in the bedroom. He shuffled into the living room dressed in his pajamas and an open robe, its cloth belt hanging from loops. He sat down and stared at the floor. He raised his head slowly and spoke first.

"For weeks now, my patients won't let me put an instrument in their mouth until I hear their opinions about our ugly world. Then they want me to respond. They need a catharsis I can't give them." He cleared his throat. "I'm tired of being isolated in a little white room with no windows and the arms of cold white dental machinery clutching at me. My own arms have become too heavy. I can hardly lift them." He looked at me for support. "Dad, I'm done."

Kelly spoke first. "You'll be broke in three months." That was my wife's hard-earned sense of financial obligation speaking.

"Maybe. I'll find a substitute fill-in dentist and then sell the practice. But as to going broke, I hardly think it will be a problem." Now his glance at me was sheepish. I held back from answering.

Kelly said, "When we lost Carol, you called every morning, and after work, you came over just to sit with me. I don't understand why you aren't doing that now for Mary."

He raised his voice just short of a cry. "Please stop with these throwaway emotions. Next you're going to say this is all God's plan, there's a deeper meaning to what's happened to all of us. Let me tell you, this is the twenty-first century, and God has some catching up to do." He looked around the room at us. "Are you listening to me? I have no answer for the people in this town. For me, I have one answer: a stiff drink."

My son, the drunken frat boy—too rich to work. He seemed intent on self-destruction. I said, "That's it. You're going to Silver Hill. It's helped people more important than you."

"Yeah, Judy Garland. Liza Minnelli. Go ahead and drop me off. When I sneak out, my drinking buddies will be waiting."

His defiance burned the blood in my veins like a medical drip. I visualized him gleefully waving a half-empty bottle of gin from the window of a careening car packed with whooping drunks. Not wanting to show how disgusted we were, Kelly and I left.

5

THE NEXT DAY I went to Trumbull Park's office in downtown Hartford. I rarely went there because I relied on my staff to watch over my hedge fund. But I had been thinking about what Sam Bixby's gun bill was up against and decided to do it, buy a controlling interest in the gun companies despite the risk. If I altered their corporate strategy and was a new voice about the easy availability of guns, that could reduce shootings. Under my control, the companies would develop and manufacture firearms required by law enforcement and the military; for the retail market, they'd sell pistols and long guns like rifles and shotguns for hunting and marksmanship. We'd add features to make them collectible. I would not allow them to sell assault rifles to civilians and would go so far as to buy up unsold inventory at distributors and gun shows. After leaving Ted's home yesterday and thinking about all that was going on, I phoned Lance Pierson, my head trader, and told him to do some research into the gun industry. I now had to sell him on the strategy, for he'd have to execute it.

"Maybe we can outflank Congressmen Bixby's opponents," I said over the phone.

I arrived at my office an hour before the market's 9:30 a.m. opening bell, hung my winter coat, and put on my old misshapen college sweatshirt. Pierson and my two other traders, Vincent and

Tracy, both in their early thirties, kept their eyes glued to the screen; this was why we maintained the office temperature at a cool sixty-five degrees, to prevent them from drowsiness. They paused long enough to nod their greetings. But when I went over to them, Pierson asked, "Is Jack doing better?" I shook my head.

Vincent said, "We're praying for him."

Pierson sat on a high-backed bar stool and the others sat flanking him on office chairs. Above them, affixed to a metal bar and tilted down, were a series of flat-panel monitors with the prices of listed American securities, commodities, and foreign currencies blinking green or red, and global news headlines from *Reuters*. I went to my glass-partitioned cubicle. Pierson followed, carrying a folder that held financial profiles of the three publicly traded American gun companies. As I received it he said, "These are the corporate valuations you wanted. After you've looked at them, I'll give you my thoughts on the plan."

Pierson had Ivy League written all over him: short, black hair, expensive black slacks, and a long-sleeved, embroidered Yale Soccer shirt. In his first ten years on Wall Street, spent at Goldman Sachs, he gained experience in risk finance involving US companies. The day he came to work for me, he ceased commuting to and from downtown Manhattan and thereby gained three hours a day at home with his wife and young children. For that, he repaid me with loyalty, and I entrusted him with the job of executing all of my investment strategies. He texted every morning before the market opened with his insights on the biggest influences on trading for the day. Once or twice a day, we exchanged texts. If I had specific instructions, I called him.

He gave me time to scan his figures before giving me his thoughts. "Their total enterprise value is about $3.9 billion. That's $2.4 billion for Krakauer Arms, $800 million for Pomeroy Weapons Group, and D.W. Swanson, the least expensive at $700 million. All three had minimal debt. Krakauer has $250 million cash on its balance sheet, so that cash will be ours to use. The others have less cash. When word of our unfriendly takeovers becomes public, the arbitrageurs will kick the shares higher, just a few points below our offering price. If you pursue this, with these three companies you'd control 75 percent of firearm production and sales. You'll be asked why."

That was an important question, and I had thought about the answer: "Some observers will see it as a philanthropic or a political act. I see it as a case of helping the local police."

The look on his face and hesitation in his voice told me he didn't like the plan. "What you want to do is nearly impossible. Three major challenges come to mind. First, the gun lobby will treat this as a direct threat. You'll be seen as taking a bite out of the Second Amendment. The NRA and the National Shooting Sports Foundation will fire up their crawlers on Capitol Hill to kill the deal. In Texas, they'll post a bounty for your arrest."

"I've already been warned about Texas."

"Second is antitrust. You're merging rivals, and that's always seen by federal regulators as bad for consumers. Too much market power in one set of hands. What you're considering has been restricted since railroad and oil barons rolled up competitors during the Gilded Age. The third hurdle is the thorniest of all: executives at these companies will fight to avoid being dislodged. It's happened before, a few years ago when the Navajo Nation wanted to buy Remington Arms, relocate factories to its reservation to give its people jobs. Even though Remington was in difficult financial straits, what seemed like a sound idea was rejected."

"We have good lawyers to help."

He had calculated the financial risk. "Finally, we'll need at least $2 billion for a 51 percent controlling stake. We'll get the $250 million of Krakauer money. We will have to borrow heavily. It's a highly leveraged deal."

"I agree with you, it's risky."

He had sound reservations, but as my lead trader, he suggested another approach that seemed feasible. "The better way is to go in with a strategic partner."

I, too, had thought of that. "I know just the person."

Bennett Durso was worth $4 billion according to Forbes Magazine. He was personally close to someone who had lost a child to a school shooting. We'd met over the years, first on the floor of the exchange, and later in Stamford on the sidelines of a presentation to high-net-worth individuals. He'd make a powerful ally. I called him and he invited me to dinner at Rao's in East Harlem. On the train ride that evening to Grand Central Station, I rehearsed how I'd present my plan. I'd bring up his comments to the media following the murder of his secretary's son when he spoke of the need for tighter restrictions on guns. I'd suggest that if we combined our capital and our stock-trading acumen, we might, over time, reduce gun violence.

As the train rolled toward the city, I thought about being a kid in Hartford. While delivering groceries from our family's Franklin Avenue store, I saw everything on the streets. I was thirteen by the summer of 1967, before eighth grade. My body was changing. The girls in class had begun wearing black fishnet stockings. A group of older boys hung out under a streetlamp, and I was sure they knew about sex and other things not taught in school.

One night, I edged toward them. One kid shunned me. "Go back to church, altar boy." Shaking that reputation wasn't going to be easy; I'd have to split the difference between what came naturally to them—their tough-guy attitude—and what came naturally to me, a curious, but clean kid. I watched them employ five-finger discounts at a variety store and return to the corner to pass around frozen juice bars or copies of Playboy. I couldn't do that; my father had the shopkeeper as a guest in our home. I also didn't care for the boys' foul language; I felt no urge to swear and didn't have the heart to belittle the fat classmate when she walked by on the sidewalk. The group slowly tolerated me, but I wanted greater acceptance. I needed to impress them.

Buster Piazza gave me an opportunity. He worked at his father's auto repair shop and possessed the tools essential to cleanly remove an ornament from the hood of a car. He asked if I'd be his lookout, and I agreed. During our first incursion downtown on a July night, we picked off several ornaments. As payment, he gave me one from a Chevrolet. It was plain, cheap, and to me, not worth the effort. My mind began working. What happened next was the first time I employed a sharp eye for material value in things, considering my eventual career as a wealth adviser and investor. I scouted the city for foreign cars and found them in the underground garages of luxury apartment buildings.

"I know where we can do better," I told Buster. We went to work, and by late August I owned a collection of stylish ornaments. One night, we showed off our trophies to the gang. I opened a towel-lined Thom McAn shoebox. Light from the streetlamp glinted off a silver leaping cat from a Jaguar, a wreathed crest from a Cadillac, and a three-pointed star from a Mercedes. Buster presented his collection, too. The kids nodded their approval. Buster gave me the credit.

"Emil went all over downtown to find these."

I reconciled my petty thievery with the appreciation that my standing in the group had been elevated. I received more than street credibility; I enjoyed the heft of these ornaments. They weren't silver or gold, just metal alloys, but I persuaded myself they would grow in value. I saw a future. To a kid of thirteen who shared a bedroom with a younger brother and a sister, the trophies represented a better life. Someday, I'd drive a Mercedes or a Cadillac up and down the avenue. I'd pull to the corner and members of a gang would clamor for a ride. They'd offer me bottles of beer or a chance to read a finger-smudged Playboy. That day would come. I hid the shoe box in the back of my dresser drawer like a squirrel hiding acorns.

By senior year in high school, I'd sprouted up above the six-foot mark. I started dating Susan Panullo. On Saturday nights, my dad gave me the keys to the family's 1971 cobalt blue Pontiac Catalina so

I could drive to the movies. Standing at her door as we headed out, she told her father that after the show, we'd stop at Friendly's for ice cream. "Won't be home too late."

But after the movie, we had sex in the Catalina's roomy back seat. Several months later, my dad sold the Catalina and bought a decrepit 1965 Dodge. It had a useful large back seat, too, yet I couldn't figure out why he traded down. But it eventually dawned on me: the nicer car had been a source of cash he needed for the family. Sales at the store, Carmen's Touch of Italy, had slipped for years. My father's Italian American clientele had been moving out to the suburbs of Wethersfield and Newington since the early 1960s, and by the 1970s, the regulars were nearly all gone. Hartford, like other American cities, was in sharp decline. Gangs peddled drugs. Burglaries and car thefts rose. South End homes were purchased by semi-skilled, hardworking Puerto Rican and Black families escaping the crime, but their diets did not include semolina wheat, deluxe cuts of salami and imported cheeses, Arborio rice, cured olives, and all the imported spices required by the Italian *Cucina*.

I noticed the changes but didn't fully understand the impact on the family business. During my first semester in college in Boston, I enjoyed the excitement of everything new, walking among the campus buildings like stone castles, meeting scores of classmates, and discussing new ideas. When I returned home for Christmas, I felt more mature. After dinner one night, I stepped from the table to the bathroom to wash. My dad evidently didn't think I could hear him. He told my mother: "The time is coming when we have to close the store."

"When must we decide?" she asked.

"One more year. We should make our plans." He added in a regretful tone: "I can find work in a butcher shop somewhere."

"We'll get by," I heard my mother say. The supper dishes clinked as she washed them. Then silence. I poked my head out of the bathroom. My father was still at the table, his hands gripping a glass of burgundy wine. My mother was looking at him. "I'll find work at one of the West Hartford supermarkets." In a rising and proud voice, she added, "Our holiday table will be as abundant as before."

I returned to the kitchen thinking maybe my presence would console my father. His eyes were clouded and perspiration darkened his face like morning dew on stone. He looked up. "Emil, pursue a career that is lucrative. We haven't said this to you or to your brother or your sister. I say it now. Money is important."

After he went out, I sat with my mother. She didn't have to repeat her husband's words. Smoke rose from her cigarette. She looked at me. "True, money would solve your father's problems. But never think money is the answer to every problem." She crushed her cigarette in an ashtray and said in a voice inflected with her view of real-world practicality. "We should pray you win the lottery."

Win the lottery? I became determined to buckle down on my education. I obtained an MBA and decided to work where the big money was, on Wall Street. The streetwise reflexes I picked up running around the South End still worked; the floor traders I went up against were a muscular, coarse crowd. But I also realized the immigrant mannerisms I carried from my old neighborhood that helped me relate to the traders wouldn't do higher up in business. I watched executives when they came to the trading floor, at receptions, and in hotel lobbies. They displayed a calm self-assurance and an earnest desire to listen. I emulated them. I improved my elocution by smoothing over my urban English and deepened my voice to a well-modulated baritone. One day, I saw an executive place a hand softly against another person's back as they turned to step away. I began to do the same. When climbing steps or entering an elevator, I gestured to others to go first. Later, when my job required a jacket and tie, I preferred solid black suits. Over time, I grew into the role; I was no longer playing at it. When I entered a room, women turned to look at me. When Kelly and I became a couple, she said I looked like Gregory Peck in *To Kill a Mockingbird*. I could see the similarities:

Mr. Peck and I were both tall, at six-foot-three, and slender, we had long, dark brown eyebrows and the same slender nose and hairline. My transformation was complete: I no longer was a scrapper from the streets of Hartford.

When the train reached Grand Central, I grabbed a cab to E. 114th Street. I'd been to Rao's twice, both times as the guest of a regular patron who owned rights to a booth one night a week. What a racket: a tiny Italian restaurant so popular that its regulars would travel uptown to E. 114th Street every week to keep a dinner slot like a timeshare. The food was average fare at best; my Aunt Connie in Waterbury used to make better homemade Italian dishes. But Aunt Connie didn't have a husband like Rao's owner and front man, Frankie. He played the host like a maitre 'd in a Hollywood movie. When I was there, I couldn't help but watch him perform; a warm and affectionate man, his smile and eyes broadened when a patron arrived. He kissed the women when they entered, and if he got to know a fellow during the night, he'd kiss him on the cheek on the way out. He turned away the uninvited with the same charm, showing them the door with his fondest wishes for good health. Frankie was a star in tailored Italian suits.

What Hollywood celebrity might I see? You'd get a seat if you were a regular, sure, but Frankie seemed to always find a booth for a famous woman or man. I got out of the cab and stepped down from the sidewalk and saw my face in Rao's front door window, and for that split moment felt I belonged. I was, after all, a billionaire. I went inside. Frankie stood there like a gatekeeper.

"Emil, yes, I recognize you. Bennett said you'd be coming." He took my outstretched hand with both of his, let it go, and led me to Durso. I noticed that Michelle Pfeiffer was sitting in a corner booth. She threw me a glance. I took it in stride.

Rao's was small. Restaurant reviewers described it as the grandfather of postwar street corner pizzerias. I inhaled aromas of roasting peppers, onions, sausages, and garlic. Jerry Vale's recording of "Amore, Scusami" arose from a vintage jukebox. Wood-framed and padded booths lined two walls. A family of eight crowded around the single table in the middle of the room; the men wore jackets and ties, and the women were in dark floral print dresses. They talked over one another as if not caring that they were easily overheard. Someone said with surprise, "She's dating a divorced man, and she still has braces? *Madonna!*" From somewhere else I heard: "Job pays New York-scale. I told you he was smart." How could an Italian family eat so much while their mouths were furiously expressing opinions? The warmhearted chatter reminded me of when my extended family gathered at the portable aluminum table my dad set up in our living room for Christmas dinner. I missed it. I missed the family-sized dishes of sliced roasts and the half-dozen side dishes. I missed the homemade wine. I missed my Aunt Anna's cakes and pies.

At his booth, Durso held his cell phone to his ear. He smiled at me and rolled his eyes in apology. I slid in across from him. Frankie handed me a menu.

"Try the broccoli rabe with garlic and red pepper flakes in EVO with any pasta. Best in the city." A waiter filled my wine glass from the bottle of Chianti that Durso had ordered. He finished his call, shook my hand, and took up his glass. "*Salute.*"

Durso was friendly and upbeat as usual, as if he couldn't hide an appreciation of his good fortune in life. He had heard about the massacre in my town. After expressing concern, he said, "To what do I owe the honor of your call?"

"I need advice. I may need money. Depends on what you think about an idea I have."

"I've heard every get-rich-quick scheme. Tell me."

"I admire you for writing checks for Brady and Giffords and other groups that advocate for gun safety. Great merit! But you and others who donate to them haven't had the success you sought." I paused to give Durso time to object, but he didn't. He instead nodded in agreement. "Why haven't you taken direct control of the industry by buying up the big manufacturers? If you did, you'd influence what they produce and whom they sell to. Could save lives." He listened intently; what I said obviously interested him. I added: "I've done the math. Fifty-one percent stakes in the big three gunsmiths would cost $2 billion. Buying them outright would run less than $4 billion. Pardon me if I'm being presumptuous, but you can afford that."

Durso signaled for a waiter, and as he gave his order I thought of the steps he'd have to take to make this a reality. He'd quietly amass a 5 percent stake in each company. That would be the easy part. At more than 5 percent, federal regulations required an investor to report his level of ownership. He'd announce his intentions and state his per-share offering price. The professionals in the market would react; arbitrageurs who made their money by buying shares of a takeover target would step in, lifting the share prices to a level a few dollars short of Durso's initial bids. In a few days, each company would issue a statement opposing the bid. Then, negotiations would quietly commence between his bankers and lawyers and the gunsmiths' bankers and lawyers. Eventually, he'd be formally turned down. His pursuit would then become unfriendly. He'd pitch his deal straight to the shareholders. He'd say how much of his own money he was using and how much he was borrowing. If we joined forces, we wouldn't have to borrow much at all. Politicians and regulators in Washington would take notice.

He waited for me to place my order, and then he surprised me. "Emil, I've already considered buying up the industry. My longtime secretary lost a son in a school shooting in Brooklyn. A fourth grader. I used to attend his birthday parties."

I nodded. "I heard about this."

He went on: "When he was killed, my staff and I turned over one idea after another and came up with the one you're suggesting now. We did the research and saw that it was a fool's errand, a needless waste of money. True, you'd end up controlling the biggest gunsmiths. But in no time at all, their 75 percent market share you controlled would shrink, and smaller private companies would gain. There are too many small gunsmiths turning out 100 to 1,000 high-quality handguns, pistols, and assault rifles a year that would love it if the big companies, those that you now owned, ceased selling certain guns commercially. They'd ramp up production to fill the void. Not only that. The skilled gunsmiths who lost jobs at your outfits would reject the non-compete clauses you asked them to sign and band together, borrow what they needed, and start up entirely new assembly lines. Among the things I learned, there is one truism: to serious gunsmiths, turning out the best firearms is both industrial art and correct politics." He drank from his glass and went on. "You'd get lots of press. Every story will quote someone praising your honorable moral stand. The article will also quote a Wall Street analyst saying you're going to lose your shirt. In a few years, you'll have lost at least 50 percent of your investment without accomplishing what you want to do—cutting down the commercial availability of those weapons. Every year at Christmas, the small companies that took over the market from you would send you a lovely card."

He'd done the analysis and I respected his conclusion. It was perhaps a lucky stroke for me. But I had to ask, "Okay. But there has to be some other way. How can someone like you and me get together and use the power of the markets?"

Bennett was several years younger. Like me, he was a second-generation Italian American. But he had inherited a fortune. His profile in Forbes described how his grandfather had arrived in Brooklyn from a Naples suburb in 1908, drove a taxi before World War I, survived six months in France, and, in peace, went back to pushing the hack. Over the first half of the twenties, he purchased more cabs, hired drivers, and parked the cars overnight on a cindered lot he owned at the corner of Flatbush Avenue and Hanson Place. In 1925, a Brooklyn-based bank searching for a place to build a new skyscraper headquarters paid him a premium for the lot. His grandfather also sold his taxi business. Flush with cash, he began building homes on mudflats in Canarsie that developers were filling in. The Durso home-building business boomed for decades. Bennett inherited $225 million in 1984 and invested in software companies like Microsoft, Oracle, and Adobe, and by the turn of the century, he was a billionaire. From that point, as a savvy investor, his wealth kept growing.

The waiter set the pasta dishes before us. Durso ordered rigatoni with vodka sauce, and I had orecchiette with broccoli rabe. In between bites and sips of wine, he suggested another way. "It's risky, but I think you have the experience to do it."

"Tell me. I'll gauge the risk."

"Sure, but before I do, I have a question, because what's at stake is not just your crusade. It's not corporate profits and losses and risking your own money. Look at it this way: if you hobble the gun companies, people will lose their jobs. You'll be taking food off their table. How do you feel about that?" He spoke with compassion. "How do you feel about imposing losses on honest investors who bought these stocks for their retirement? You'll inflict collateral damage on people who simply have a different opinion from you. It will be as if you're taking the law into your own hands."

I had already thought over how I'd be portrayed as a corporate raider, a pirate who didn't care about job losses. I carefully framed my answer. "I don't want any of those things to happen. But tell me, what law am I breaking? If any, I'll call it quits. You think the morality behind my intent is vengeance for my grandson's coma and for killing my neighbors' children? It's not. My moral authority is using the power of money for what I see as a widespread public good."

"One more question. How much are you willing to lose?"

"Nearly everything not set aside in trusts. That would leave me $25 million to live on."

His cell phone sounded. "My apologies. I have to take this call."

I looked past Durso and overheard Frankie welcoming a family of four: parents with a teenage son and daughter. Everyone was formally dressed, the males in dark blue blazers and ties, the females in long skirts. Frankie knew them and turned on the charm. He took both of the woman's hands in his and kissed her gently on the cheek. He glanced at the son and daughter: The young boy and girl were beautiful. The boy's hair was stylishly long and the girl was very pretty. They didn't have teenage facial blemishes. Frankie said: "Michael has the look of a Fortune 500 CEO. Cynthia, too, if she passes on Hollywood." The kids could have been Ted and Carol. Kelly and I had heard the same adoring words about our children wherever we arrived as guests. Frankie escorted this family to a booth. I watched the father walk behind his family. I didn't need X-ray vision to know his heart swelled with satisfaction. That man once was me.

Durso finished his call. "As I was saying, right, put that $25 million securely away." He lowered his voice to add, "You could try to corner production of gunpowder, but bandit labs would pop up, just like with illegal drugs. Bullets too. Instead, this is what you do. Short the hell out of the shares of the big three. Pin their prices down to single digits and keep 'em there as long as you can. You have experience running a long-short hedge fund, right? Make it difficult for the companies to raise capital. Stifle their balance sheets. Over time, they'll struggle to reinvest in plant and equipment, product development, and marketing. You'll bring attention to how their profits every year are lumpy, and other market players will pile on. After all, these companies are pariahs. Rock-bottom stock valuations should work for a while until the politicians in Washington finally wake up." He took a drink of wine. "But be careful. You can lose millions in a short squeeze in a heartbeat."

"You're not suggesting I short and distort these stocks?"

"No. Just stick with the facts. What you're doing could be a catastrophe for the gun companies."

"I can do that. Shorting shares was my first big lesson in the market. I made $20,000 on one shrewd play. Seems puny now, but it was big in 1982."

This made Durso smile. "Okay, but it's a more dangerous game today because of how swiftly things are done online. The young traders at WallStreetBets are prowling for shorts to squeeze, and they'll eat you alive."

On the train ride home, I considered Durso's advice. Following it would contradict everything I'd done during my professional life. For forty years on Wall Street, I cheered on the capital markets as a trader on the exchange floor, an investment adviser to high-net-worth families, and as part owner of a hedge fund. But since the massacre, life had irrevocably changed; if I followed his suggestion, I was going to try to cripple the finances of three American companies.

Yet was I an impostor? Were my intentions truly unselfish and did I honestly think I could achieve what eluded the nation's leaders in Washington, with the goal of reducing gun violence in America? Was I now in a conspiracy with Durso? Was I leaching onto his idea to succeed, or was it nothing more than a shrewdly concocted charade to atone for my late-in-life misgivings about my gun investments? Kelly would help me find the answers. At dinner the next evening, I shared Durso's ideas with her. She was unconvinced of their merits. I tried to reassure her, but she wouldn't have it.

"Don't do this," she fumed. "This isn't the right way to help your family recover." I rehashed the argument, but she wouldn't have it. After dinner, she went off to our bedroom. I followed her, but she would not discuss it further.

The argument resumed at breakfast. She was sipping coffee in the kitchen when I joined her. She lowered her cup, placed it in both palms, and looked at me directly. "So what does your conscience say today?"

"The same thing it said last night." I sat back so Mila could pour me a cup. "This is not a vanity project. This is something I must try to do."

"What about our last years together? This will absorb your time."

Mila placed a cup of granola before me. She headed toward the laundry. For twenty-four years, our maid had kept confidential every harsh word that infiltrated our home. Her eyes never met those of the combatants, though she overheard every salvo. Her dispassion reminded me to remain calm. I spooned fresh-cut strawberries and blueberries into my bowl. "Things have changed. We can't sail away on another posh vacation while Jack and Ted are clinging to life back in Connecticut."

"I agree. I'll help Mary no matter what happens. Jack may need permanent care. Ted's therapy will be enormously expensive. Did you forget that he and Mary will have difficulty paying for medical insurance? Take all this into account." She sighed heavily, looked away and then back to me. "It feels like I'm back in Kew Gardens and I hear my mother agonizing with my father about the mortgage. Emil, I'm not young anymore. I can't take this." Then she shocked me. "I don't want to be poor again."

"I'm not going to squander away everything. I'll set aside $25 million. If I lose the rest, I can make that amount grow. If something were to happen to me, you'll have more than enough."

I went to her, and she softened in my embrace but wasn't entirely at ease. "Why take on this risk? Why not leave this to the people who run the country? I'm so tired of this cycle of grief, car accidents, opioids, and mass shootings. Isn't anyone in charge?"

I kissed her forehead, her cheek, and her lips and said, "We thought we were better than the countless millions of parents in the Third World who watch their children die of malnutrition and get caught up in tribal warfare. The only thing that's different is our problems, the guns and drugs and suicides. Everyone carries on the best way they can. But for me, I feel that what's happened in town has helped me take hold of myself. This is what I want to do, and we're fortunate that we can do it. I need your support."

6

A WEEK LATER, I sat at our trading desk with my staff before the stock market's opening. Pierson and I had devised a plan around Durso's suggestion of selling the gunsmiths' shares short to slash their value. We'd borrow shares from the big Wall Street brokerages and sell them, and continue borrowing and selling them over the next week. The average daily trading volume of Krakauer Arms was a million shares, and the other two companies, D.W. Samson and Pomeroy Weapons Group, about 500,000. These volumes were tiny compared to the millions of shares traded each day in big tech names like Alphabet and Apple and old-line blue chips like IBM and Bank of America. A small number of shares in circulation made it easier to move the price of the stock. Selling shares short required an interested buyer, and there just wasn't a horde of investors interested in owning gun stocks. To knock them down to $10 a share or lower was going to take time and patience, but my staff and I could do it. From experience, I knew we'd eventually trade short 40 to 50 percent of each company's outstanding shares, maybe more. Over time, we'd buy them back at lower prices for a profit and return the borrowed shares to the brokerage. I wouldn't do that for a while. I intended to pin the prices lower for several months. By then, there might be a chain reaction: other investors might pile on or one of the companies might go bankrupt. Maybe Washington would react with helpful legislation. I'd watch and wait.

"They'll know it's us," Pierson said.

"Trade through Drakeford."

Pierson phoned Drakeford Capital, my longtime institutional broker, and put the call on speakerphone. "At the open, start selling short 5,000 share blocks of Samson and Pomeroy," he told a Drakeford trader. "Keep at it all week until you knock the prices down to eight or nine a share. Also, short 10,000 share blocks of Krakauer until it's down to ten."

The trader asked, "What if the decline is so swift we trip the limit down circuit breaker?" That was a stock market safety measure designed to prevent panic selling.

"Take the required break. The floor specialists generally digest in fifteen minutes what's happening when a circuit breaker trips. When the stocks resume trading, go at them again."

We watched CNBC live markets coverage. At 9:30 a.m., the sound of the opening bell echoed around the white-marbled walls of the cavernous exchange. The overall market rose but the gunsmiths' shares began blinking red on our screens. Within fifteen minutes, the shares of all three gunsmiths fell 8 percent. The anchors on CNBC picked up on this. "The firearm manufacturers are down today," one said. "Has an influential Wall Street analyst downgraded the entire industry?"

Another said, "Maybe one company is going bankrupt?"

"That's possible. Colt and Remington went bankrupt a few years ago before being bought up by larger companies to revive the brands. Manufacturers and distributors have taken on too much debt and are stuck with unsold inventory. If one is in trouble, we'll hear about it. Stay tuned."

Over the years I'd seen smart long-term investors keep an eye out for stocks that fell below a company's fundamental value, and when that happened, they jumped in and picked up shares at the low price. That's what happened to our targets: the gunsmiths slid lower and then stabilized when buyers came in to buy them. Traders at Drakeford Capital watched for this to happen. To prevent a true bounce back in price, they resumed the short selling. The failure of the gun stocks to stabilize in price eroded any residual confidence these long-term investors had in them. Eroding this confidence was critical to my plan.

To bring in some income, I built another facet into Durso's strategy. During the session, Pierson sold naked call options traded in Chicago on the shares. Naked calls meant Trumbull Park didn't own the shares. Selling calls, almost always to a professional trader, obligated me to buy the gunsmiths' shares if they jumped in price within a set time, usually a week or two, perhaps as long as a month. I gave myself plenty of safety by choosing a very high price at which the obligation would kick in. If the stocks didn't reach that price, the option would expire and I'd pocket the income from selling it. Since my short selling was pounding the shares lower, the probability that they would rise to my option price was slim to none. They'd spring higher, defeating my strategy, if unforeseen positive news broke such as if a suitor emerged to buy Krakauer or if it received a colossal new contract. This seemed remote; unrelenting gun violence had reduced nearly all investors interested in the industry.

At the end of the day, the stocks closed down. Krakauer had fallen to $14 a share from $22, Pomeroy and Samson settled at $11 a share, down from $16. At the end of the week, they were even lower. By then, Trumbull Park had shorted 30 percent of the shares available to trade. To exercise this strategy, stock market regulators required me to set aside $300 million. I put up $150 million of Trumbull Park money and borrowed another $150 million. During the next week, Pierson and the traders at Drakeford kept the pressure on the beaten-down stocks. I enjoyed a quiet moment of triumph.

But my triumph was short-lived. In no time, Clayton Jeffries heard about the attack on the gunsmiths. A gun enthusiast in Virginia who was a fellow member of the NRA complained bitterly by phone that his shares in Krakauer Arms had cratered to $10. Distressed by this news, Jeffries ordered his chief of staff to check it out. Despite my use of Drakeford to mask my trading, this staffer learned from Wall Street contacts that Trumbull Park had beaten down Krakauer shares. When told this, Jeffries placed an irate call to Bixby. I had not warned Bixby before initiating my plan, so Jeffries's invective surprised him. He recorded Jeffries's call. That night he called me to say he was flying up from Washington and wanted to come straight to the house. I asked why, and he answered that something I had done had gone terribly wrong.

When he arrived, Bixby let loose: "Why didn't you warn me about what you were doing? I had to hear it first from Jeffries." He waved away Mitchell's offer of a drink and placed his micro recorder on the kitchen counter. He fumbled with the playback button but finally hit it.

Jeffries was apoplectic. "Sam, you're a skunk. You don't have the votes, so you put your billionaire friend up to devalue the gun industry."

"What are you talking about?"

"I'm talking about a hedge fund that sighted in on gun stocks and is going for the kill. It's the work of Trumbull Park. That's your friend Scordato."

"Emil's a free agent. He can do whatever he wants."

"Don't lie to me," Jeffries barked. "Admit it. You're using him. This is a clever attack to weaken Second Amendment rights. At least the Hollywood liberals and university health researchers play by the rules and hire lobbyists and Madison Avenue to attack us. But your man has gone rogue, trying to bankrupt a patriotic industry." He wheezed into the phone and tried to catch his breath. "I'll rally every conservative financier behind me. I call my friends at the Pentagon. I'll smoke him out and kill him."

"Clayton, just hold on. Just wait for me to look into this."

Jeffries wasn't reassured. He knew how to pressure Bixby. "I told you both when you were standing in my living room and drinking my bourbon, and I'll say it again. When your bill comes before the full House in April, I won't let it pass." He ended the call.

I apologized to Bixby. "I'm surprised he found out so quickly."

Bixby ceased seething. He turned to Mitchell and now wanted that glass of bourbon. "How did you attack the gun industry?" I went over how my short-selling strategy worked and why it would help us. He acknowledged that we had very briefly discussed something like this, though he now expressed concern. "Can't you lose big money? What kind of countermeasure does Jeffries have?"

"Everyone in the market knows these are stodgy stocks. I doubt he can drum up buyer interest to force them higher. Pierson watches our positions every waking moment. I'm not worried at all."

7

IT WAS MARCH. Ted had not entered rehab. He was fighting his addiction to drink. On a pleasant Sunday afternoon that had signs of spring, he and Mary took a drive. They stopped for lunch at a roadhouse. Afterward, she told me, "He ordered a soda, not a gin and tonic. I pretended to take no notice." I was happy for them and for Kelly and me. All of us were due a break. Ted might reconsider returning to his practice. He might be better prepared for Jack's outcome, good or bad. I felt relieved.

It was a hopeful moment that did not last. His body rebelled with the symptoms of withdrawal. The doctor had warned Mary to expect this and explained these symptoms were the body's way of healing. For several evenings, his hands shook, his pulse raced, and he felt nauseous. In bed, he broke out in cold sweats. When Mary held him close, she felt the stress in his body. Ted had difficulty getting comfortable and could not sleep, and his inability to rest eventually defeated him. After less than a week of pitching feverishly in the middle of the night, he began getting up. An hour later he returned to bed and slept until mid-morning.

Then Mary called me in a panic. "When he got up again last night, I crept quietly to the bottom of the stairs to watch. He was in the kitchen. He stood at the liquor cabinet and lifted a bottle of gin straight up and chugged from it. He gasped to catch his breath. He took a few more sips. When he recapped the bottle, I crept back upstairs."

I visualized Ted rushing the bottle to his lips and sucking hard. "Did he come right back to bed?"

"A bit later. I was still awake. I asked him if he was all right. He said he was. He said he had been sitting on the couch waiting to become sleepy again. He was calm. He settled back to sleep quickly. He's still asleep."

"You haven't confronted him. Okay. While he's asleep, clear the house of every bottle."

That afternoon, the four of us, Mary and Ted, Kelly and me, met at Jack's bedside. We stood around not saying much. Jack had received the same care for two months. I took his hand, held it securely, and watched his respiratory action. I mumbled, "Jack, we're here. Jack, we're praying for you." Kelly, Mary, and I were clinging to hope. Not Ted. When he held his son's hand, Ted's facial skin seemed to turn a hue of purple, so dark that the tears that rolled down his cheeks did not glisten.

We had asked Dr. Bertrand to meet us. When he arrived he confirmed: "There's been no improvement."

Ted asked him a question that was stated as fact: "He can remain in a coma for years."

"That's true."

"He can die."

"That too. But keep believing he comes out of it. He needs you on his side."

That was it. We were told again to wait. Driving home, I wondered about the doctor's approach. I understood he couldn't make false promises and assure a positive outcome. But surely telling us to hope had its limitations. At a red light, I looked out and wondered what it was about the word 'hope' that touches the brain and the heart. I remembered a line in Scripture that teaches the afflicted that their sufferings produce an endurance and character that engenders hope. Okay, I got it. But I doubted if there was a lesson on hope in the medical textbooks, even though doctors relied on hope like a stethoscope. Doctors didn't convey hope with a right to pursue legal recourse if it failed to deliver. It wasn't offered with a timeframe. If it were, then Wall Street analysts would study the predictions markets and ponder the prophecies of war and famine and assign hope an interest rate, and before trading on it, investors and money managers would have to weigh its duration risk. In everyone's life, every morning is filled with hope that things will be better than the day before. Hope lifts the spirits of patients and their families, but it too often vanishes into eternity.

At lunch the next day, Mitchell placed a copy of the *Hartford Courant* at my usual seat, folded to a story about an assault on a wealthy Connecticut Gold Coast couple in their home. I picked it up and read it. Two gunmen had studied the man's routine and had hidden in the bushes on the well-lit grounds of his mansion to hold him and his wife up as they stepped out of their car. They then forced their way into the house. The robbers knew the couple's staff was off at that hour. The case made the newspaper only after the gunmen were apprehended. A detective quoted in the story said assaults like this were occurring with an unsettling frequency in Gold Coast communities. "They're difficult to prevent."

I showed the story to Kelly and thanked Mitchell for bringing it to our attention. "We have a very sophisticated electronic sentry system. What are you thinking?"

"If professionals defeated our security system like they did that one, and they had guns, you and Mrs. Scordato would be at risk. I'd step between them and you. I owe you that much. But I'd feel better if my handgun were here in the house."

"Absolutely not. You know how I've come to feel about guns."

"With respect, sir, I also know how you feel about Mrs. Scordato."

When we moved to Todd's Chapel, I didn't think I'd ever need a gun to keep my family safe. The property had a security system and the town was far removed from the everyday crime in Hartford, Bridgeport, or New Haven. Now that the question of bringing a gun into the home was before me, I detested the idea. Mitchell was politely insistent.

"I'd be very willing to receive the proper training."

Mitchell's family owned a sheep farm in Victoria north of Melbourne amid rolling pastures and acres of woods. He was his father's main station hand, riding on horseback to check fences and prod sheep from the field to a paddock. He carried a pistol to shoot snakes. For pleasure, he used a rifle to shoot wild pigeons and rabbits. He had told me: "I was a competent shot at ten meters with a pistol and a longer distance with a rifle." He'd brought his handgun to America and kept it hidden in his garage apartment at our home.

As I ate lunch, I thought about Mitchell's suggestion. We were his American family, and he was committed to protecting us. I looked over as he polished tumblers and other glasses and considered his offer to undergo training. He was mentally and emotionally stable. To stow a gun securely in the house felt like a rational decision, even more so in an irrational environment where guns outnumber the 330 million people in this country. I beckoned him over.

"If you used your gun in this house, are you willing to live with the possibility of killing someone?"

He thought for a moment and said with conviction: "In service to my employer, yes. I'd see it as my obligation and my right."

Kelly sided with Mitchell. "Emil, he'll bring his lock box in from his apartment. No one would know where it was but us."

I sat back. We were all under enormous stress. My home was a rich target for professional thieves, and I wanted to feel a sense of control and peace. A home invasion was at least a destiny I could prevent. But the moral quandary of bringing a gun into my home was something I just could not bridge.

I said to them, "It's easy to imagine Mitchell getting the drop on an armed intruder. Hollywood can write that scene into its scripts.

But my gut tells me something would go wrong, and more likely, a gun here would assure us that blood would stain our floors, and we'd always hear the echoes of gunfire. I'd rather update our security system so that every time the front gate is activated, the grounds light up like a ballpark and a chime sounds in the front hall. I may have come late to this awareness of guns, but I'll have none in our home."

My ploy to sweep Ted's home and clear the bottles of gin didn't last. One night, he went out drinking. It was the first Monday in April, and the Men's NCAA championship basketball game was on. I'd invited him over to watch it, but he said he preferred to stay home. I offered him company, but he said he didn't think he'd watch the whole game. Not watch the entire NCAA finals? That sounded suspicious, but I let it go. My son lied to me. Hours before tipoff, he went to a restaurant and sat at the bar. In Todd's Chapel, my besotted son's habits were well known. During the first half of the game, a bartender called my house phone. Mitchell answered, and he brought the phone to me. The bartender said, "Ted's here and he's soused. He's nearly passed out."

The restaurant was close enough for Mitchell and me to reach it during half-time. Ted had cradled his head into the crook of his arms on the counter. The bartender said, "I offered him coffee, but he waved me away."

I paid the tab generously, and Mitchell and I helped my son to stand and walk. We drove in silence. Once at his home, I settled with Ted in front of his television to watch the final minutes of the game. He struggled to speak. "Jus' like her husband! That's what Grandma Lilly said. I was just like her husband, a useless drunk."

"When did she say that?"

"During Joanne's wedding. Remember, at the hotel in Danbury? I was drinking with cousins Michael and Leo in the parking lot. We were telling stories and laughing like college kids. Hell, we were college kids. I tipped a waiter so he'd keep bringing us drinks, and Grandma followed him out." Slurring his words, Ted mimicked the voice of

Kelly's mother. "She shouted, 'You three. Come back inside. Ted, you're a useless drunk just like my husband.' I said to her, 'We're having fun here. So, what!' But she was right, Dad. I admit it. I like my sauce."

He offered an insight into his need to drink. "I won't say that you spoiled me. I had everything and I never needed anything. All I wanted was to be happy. Drinking leaves me with no worries." He paused for a second and joked, "Thank heavens I never tried heroin or crack."

I've been giving advice to him for years, but as I looked over at him, it didn't seem that it did much good. It struck me to try something different, maybe achieve some kind of breakthrough. I decided to tell him about my wild nights in Manhattan.

"I've had moments of excess, too," I began. He looked hard at me. "When I was in my late twenties before I met your mother, I did cocaine every week."

"Did Mom know?"

"She did, because she was the one who broke me of the habit. Coke was popular among traders in the 1980s. It wasn't just for ballplayers and musicians. The same colleagues who would later help me make millions of dollars in distressed corporate debt and oil stocks introduced me to it. We'd meet at Harry's after the closing, drink single malt Scotch, eat, and talk about our investments. Then we'd go to my buddy Oliver's place in Chelsea and do coke. We'd go out to a disco somewhere, usually on Varick Street. Oliver would arrange for high-end hookers to meet us. We had the money. We were driven to live big before settling down."

Ted's eyes were wide. He sat up higher on the sofa as though he were sobering up. I went on. "My steady date every Monday night was with Vivienne. A tall beauty with a French accent. We'd end up at my place. High on coke, she could go all night. Two hundred bucks, plus tip and cab fare home."

"Holy shit. How old were you?"

"Twenty-eight, twenty-nine. I was a zombie on Tuesdays. Once I fell asleep on the subway and missed my stop. I wasn't naive, though.

I tried to keep my wits about me and I never woke up in a strange room. I always showed up at the exchange the next day. We lived flamboyantly, but we were also driven to make money."

"How'd you pull out of it?"

"I met your mother. That was my chance to stop, and that's what I'm saying to you now. Something positive happened to shake me out of it. Now you're facing a crisis. There's still a way out. Do it for Jack."

He looked down and shook his head. "If he recovers. What if he doesn't?"

"He will wake up. You'll have fun teaching him to drive. He'll become a fine young man. He might need permanent care. Heck, he may even wrestle again. Never worry about the expense. Your mother and I will give you everything you need." Ted still looked glum. I decided to tell him about another concern. "Should Jack die, and unless you and Mary have another boy, the Scordato name disappears. I was mistaken to not place our family name on the hospital wing or the new sports complex. I'm leaving nothing to hang a worthy legacy on."

"You've given to the church. The bishop should name something for you, a school or a social hall."

"Maybe. But after what I've just told you about my own addictions, I'm not lobbying for it. So why don't we both think of something to hang the family name on."

This, I thought, was something for him to look forward to.

8

MY EFFORTS WITH TED FELL FLAT. Several mornings later, Mary called again, this time at 6 a.m. "He's drinking grain alcohol," she said in a panic. "The cleaning lady bought it to wipe down surfaces during the pandemic. A leftover bottle was stored on the Lazy Susan with the other kitchen cleaners under the kitchen counter. I caught him drinking it in the middle of the night again."

That was poison at 190 proof. "Pour it out."

"It's a big bottle that's nearly empty."

That was it. Mary didn't ask explicitly, but Ted needed to detoxify. I called Silver Hill to make preparations for rehab, whether or not he resisted.

The next morning, it was Pierson who called at 6:45 a.m. He only called that early when a fast decision was needed—usually a rare opportunity to make money. This time, we needed to cut our losses. I groped for my cell phone on the night table.

"The Pentagon arranged for Krakauer to get a huge $100 million NATO contract. The stock is indicated to open at more than double yesterday's closing price of ten. No telling how much higher it goes between now and when regular trading begins," he said. The words were like a thunderclap. I swung my legs out from beneath the covers and began to rub my thigh vigorously. He said. "I didn't wait for Drakeford. I began placing orders to buy back the shares we sold short. We're going to start the day millions in the red."

Trumbull Park was going to get run over. "That's right, cut our losses before the Chicago options players hear about this." If those traders began purchasing Krakauer call options, there was no limit to how high the stock could go. Veteran floor traders always avoided short squeezes like the one we were experiencing because they knew that with the leverage of call options, a shorted stock could rise to infinity. I did not want to become intimate with infinity. "Close out our options contracts, too."

The other gunsmiths were also indicated higher, rising in sympathy with Krakauer. Pierson knew to close out our shorts with them as well. I was going to lose tens of millions of dollars. I didn't like it, but I could survive that level of loss.

I went to my computer and called up Krakauer Arms' website to see what it said about the NATO contract. After the bureaucratic verbiage about improving relations with NATO, a news release gave the meat of the story: At the Pentagon's urging, troops from Sweden and Finland, the alliance's newest members, would be outfitted with the company's standard assault rifle during an upcoming exercise in the Baltic Sea, on the island of Gotland, which sat between Saint Petersburg and the Russian enclave of Kaliningrad. "This makes it a highly valuable target in any conflict with Moscow. The exercise, hosted by Sweden, is designed to preserve the freedom of navigation," the statement said. Krakauer noted that the contract would be very profitable. The first $50 million in weapons would be shipped immediately from inventory, so that revenue would go straight to the bottom line as profit. Krakauer would get another $50 million in a year when NATO exercised an option for the delivery of more rifles.

The story said that key members of Congress had promoted the deal. It did not give Jeffries's name. But I knew.

I called up the online Reddit discussion forum to read the chatter: "Memestock Megathread for this morning. Heavily shorted arms maker reprieved by big NATO order." That was it. Online traders that hunt for stocks that had been beaten down by short selling were snapping up the gunsmiths' shares.

Even as daylight came, Pierson had pounded out orders on his laptop. In a frenzied thirty minutes covering our shorts, we lost $120 million. Then, with the start of regular market trading, our loss approached $200 million. There was no getting around what had happened: I failed to heed Durso's warning and focused only on what could go right and dismissed all that could go wrong. I felt stupid for not placing offsetting hedges to my positions. Later that day, *Reuters*' stock market coverage said that a NATO contract had lifted Krakauer's stock higher. My heart sank when the story publicized what I would have preferred to keep private: "Hedge fund Trumbull Park took a drubbing, losing at least $200 million."

I was no longer a billionaire.

9

I'VE READ THAT THE SPIRIT, like the body, can heal itself without magic foods or religious intercession, relying on a rising self-awareness that might help a broken person see what can be made right. Depression runs a course like sleep, and just as the rising sun wakes us up, a new idea or positive event can help a depressed person see the light. That's what I tried to tell Ted the night of the NCAA game, that he should watch for some kind of positive change. But Ted never made it to Silver Hill.

Kelly's cell phone rang in the middle of the night. Mary was calling from the emergency room. Ted had been vomiting and overcome by nausea at home, and she'd rushed him to the hospital. Within an hour, we joined her in a waiting room. Several hours later, an ER doctor gave us the grim news that several of Ted's organs were failing. The medical staff was doing all it could, and Dr. Bertrand was on his way. We were allowed to see Ted. He lay in bed on life support with an oxygen mask tube running to his face. We milled uncomfortably around waiting for the doctor, not able to sit and not saying much to one another. Dr. Bertrand arrived and first received a status report from his ER colleagues. Then he went straight to Mary. "I'm sorry," he said. He turned to Kelly and me with a look of mourning. "Abusive drinking damaged his liver and has progressively led to acute organ failure."

What I predicted months before to him had come to pass: the bottom had dropped out. "Can't you give him a transplant?" I asked.

"A transplant is considered in many cases of acute liver failure." He looked at Mary. "But not in Ted's case."

I resented this answer. Where was his compassion for Mary? The doctor knew who I was. He knew what my family had done for the hospital, how many millions we'd given. I felt a rising outrage. I scowled at him. Dr. Bertrand remained calm and said nothing, and I realized he was giving me time to process it all. He had an obligation to be straight and not offer false hope. Despite my generosity, I had no claim on the hospital's services, no degree of entitlement. I could not demand that its staff extend themselves beyond standard procedures. People died in hospitals every day. There was no grim reaper I could challenge, just bodily failure.

After a moment he said: "Normally, we'd assess his eligibility for a transplant. We'd assess whether he's well enough to survive the surgery and recover. If we had confidence he could beat his alcohol addiction, it might give us reason to try. But Ted has a long history, and more than his liver is in jeopardy. His kidneys are gone. His intestines are perforated and have filled his abdomen with fluid."

My son was going to die.

Kelly held Mary as they both wept. I slumped in a chair and took my head in both hands. If Ted were to live, I'd give up everything. I sucked in a deep breath to try to compose myself. My mother was right so long ago about what money could not do; it meant nothing at the moment of imminent death.

What more could Dr. Bertrand do? What came next? My thoughts jumped to my grandson lying in a different intensive care unit in a coma. I looked up at the doctor. Our eyes fixed on one another in silence, and then in that deepening quiet that occurs between two people aware they're thinking the same thing, we remembered that Jack was still living. In a quivering voice, I asked: "Do you think my grandson will live?"

"Didn't the nurse tell you? Late yesterday there was some arousal. We pinched his pinky, and he moved it away. We're detecting faster electronic pulses. His chances are improving."

I went to Ted. "Did you hear that? Jack is going to make it."

A nurse stood respectfully just outside the door to Ted's room. The doctor went to her, and they conversed quietly. He left, and she went to Mary. "You may want to have people come in to say goodbye. Let us know when it's time."

She had chosen her words carefully. Better than telling Mary, "Let your husband go."

10

WE BURIED TED on a Wednesday. Father Rushmore said at the funeral Mass, "It took three months, but the gymnasium killer claimed another victim, though not by gunfire. There may be others."

I was glad he kept the service brief, for we were flying to Washington later in the afternoon to join 250 people who had boarded buses at several points in Connecticut that morning to watch the final debate and vote on Bixby's bill in the House of Representatives the next day. Before we could leave, Kelly and I went to Mary's home to join a gathering of mourners. I acknowledged our thanks to our friends with a brief chitchat or, in one or two cases, a smile and a nod from across the room. As the afternoon wore on, I could see Kelly was exhausted. So was I. I felt relieved when I received a text from the driver of our hired car telling us he was waiting outside to take us to the airport. But our long day was far from over.

Kelly asked, "Do we need to be in Washington just to watch Sam lose? We have an obligation here. I don't want to leave Mary alone."

It was true Sam hadn't given himself much of a chance, but I felt I should be there, not only for our friends and for him, but to personally see this to the end. Before I could tell this to Kelly, Mary stepped over. She urged us to go: "I'm okay. I'm surrounded by friends."

Kelly fell asleep as soon as she reclined in the comfortable seat of a small private jet. I watched her. When we were engaged, we talked about the family we would have. She wanted only two kids; she didn't think she could provide the proper care if we had more than two. I agreed and assured her everyone in the family would be safe. I didn't imagine the forces outside of our control. Thinking of this depressed me, and thankfully, I, too, nodded off. We both awakened when the jet landed, and we jumped into a cab at Reagan Airport. Evening traffic was heavy in Washington, but we arrived at a Marriott hotel just as people were stepping off the buses. Bixby and his staff greeted everyone. It was a diverse group of parents of slain students and teachers, survivors, friends, and educators; they took luggage to their rooms and then converged in the hotel lounge for dinner and drinks. Many were excited to be in Washington. A few thought mass shootings that winter and early spring would get Bixby and his co-sponsors the votes they needed.

"We're going to witness history this week," said Fletcher Lowell. "Approval in the House, then on to the Senate for passage and to the Oval Office for the president's signature."

Bixby tried to temper the enthusiasm. He was too realistic to feel encouraged that a mass shooting in a Nashville school earlier in the week would change the minds of even one House colleague. He explained that to us and added that even as he worked the bill through committee, he was forced to drop the ban on assault rifles. With this dilution demanded by House conservatives, the bill was approved and sent to the full House for Thursday's vote.

"We'll be voting on what I really wanted, the repeal of the federal liability shield," he said. "An assault weapons ban is a Second Amendment fight for some future time."

We sat with him at dinner. "We're at least three votes short," he said. "Clyde Sutter from Kansas is on the fence. Clayton Jeffries is avoiding me. He won't talk to me. When we're in close proximity on the floor, he looks away. His chief of staff won't take our phone calls. I know he gave the bill serious study."

Jeffries, the windbag, wouldn't talk? Money may not have meant anything to him, and his re-election didn't depend on his vote. But I sensed an opportunity. I decided to try to reason with him. I knew where he lived. I pushed away my plate and waited for Bixby to turn away and become deep in discussion with someone. I said to Kelly, "I'm going to Georgetown."

"Why?"

"To pick up an ornament." She didn't know what I meant, and I didn't have time to explain.

The cab driver headed for O Street. Would Jeffries be home? It was pushing 9 p.m. Would he be up? In the darkness of the rear seat, I considered my approach. He was too sophisticated, too wise to the ways of negotiation, so I'd have to go at it straight and make a direct appeal.

When the driver turned onto O Street, I asked him to slow down so that I could spot Jeffries's home. Our passage was narrowed by luxury cars lining both sides of the street. I recognized the window that had been lit up by firelight the late afternoon that Bixby and I had visited, though the window was dark. As I stepped out onto the sidewalk, luxury car hood ornaments glinted in the lamplight as if beckoning me, but I passed them by. I knocked on his door. His butler let me in and offered to take my coat. I shook my head. "I'll only be a minute." I waited in the hallway.

Without the scent of wood smoke from a blazing fireplace, the air in his home was heavy with the funk of age and cigars. Jeffries greeted me in a velvet red smoking jacket with an Asian design and spill stains. He carried a lit cigar.

"Heavens, Emil. There must be something terribly wrong for you to be here so late. What is it?"

I thanked him with a slight smile. "I'm here to ask a favor."

"May I offer you something?" He motioned with his cigar toward his butler who stood nearby. I shook my head. He gestured to the parlor for me to sit, but I waved him off. "Then how may I help?"

"You lost a son in Iraq."

"Yes, Billy, my only son. He was a VMI graduate and had earned a captain's rank in the Army. We were close. Sara and I are thankful we have our daughters."

"Billy died for his country, for a cause?"

"I believe so, yes."

"I lost my only son too. Ted died a few days ago. We buried him today before leaving for Washington. It wasn't a violent death, like your son's. We just turned the oxygen off."

He dropped his hands to his side as if yielding. His voice softened. "I'm terribly sorry to hear this."

"He might as well have died alongside all of the others in the gymnasium. The longer his son Jack lay in a coma, the worse it was for Ted. He drank himself to death." My voice nearly cracked; I was sure he detected a tremor in it when I said, "I want to believe Ted also lost his life for a cause. That will happen if Bixby's bill is approved." I waited, but Jeffries said nothing. "You voted for the Iraq War and gave your son to it. You remember him as a hero. I remember my son as a victim. Your vote for Bixby can change that."

Jeffries said nothing, in keeping with Bixby's description that he could respond with a mute silence. I turned to leave. "Thank you for your time."

He saw me to the door. Nearer to me, I sensed a whiff of whiskey. He said: "If Sam loses by a vote or two, a very narrow defeat like that in the House means the bill remains viable. He can come right back and resubmit it. He shouldn't lose hope."

I nodded my thanks again, both to him and his butler, and left. I walked a few blocks to M Street. I stood alone, needing a moment to think. Patrons were straggling out of a Georgetown restaurant where the window still blazed. Jeffries had kept his vote close to his vest. But in the final moment, he offered encouragement, and that had to be enough. My thoughts began to clear. I had made an honest effort. What I tried these last few months was all that I could think to do. I ordered an Uber, the car arrived quickly. As the car drove on, it seemed that tomorrow's vote by all those strangers on the House floor would be as much a judgment of me as it would be about Sam's legislation. I could accept that. I began to relax, and by the time I reached the hotel, all of my built-up expectations and the tension from self-recrimination had uncoiled. I felt free of them.

The next day, the Todd's Chapel contingent of 250 sat together in a full House gallery to witness the vote. After several speeches, Bixby's co-sponsor from Colorado, Representative Bettina Gray, stepped to the lectern.

"For years in the Middle East, at a Ramallah bus stop, at an Israeli kibbutz, and during the war in Gaza, lives were shattered by bombings and gunfire that are so endemic to everyday life that the Palestinians and Israelis end every conversation with a petition to God, 'May God's mercy keep you safe.' Spontaneous spasms of slaughter have also come to Colorado. You've heard of Columbine, of Aurora, of King Soopers, and of Club Q. As we go about our daily lives, knowing this threat can strike at any moment, we will soon be petitioning God for safety from gun violence.

"When we debate here in Congress, we repeat tired phrases like 'Enforce the laws that exist,' and 'Close the gun show loophole,' or 'You can't stop people from committing suicide.' So we cook up pap we think will go down easy with the gun lobby. The NRA spits it out anyway, and so do its friends sitting in this chamber. But if spectacular school massacres such as in Todd's Chapel and in Nashville rivet our attention, then I say, seize the moment." She sat down to a smattering of applause from her side of the chamber.

Ellis Middleton, a conservative member from South Carolina, spoke next. "To simplify why law-abiding Americans reject any restrictions on guns, I'll tell you about Charlton Heston. You know him well, not only as Moses in *The Ten Commandments* but for a decade as the high priest of gun rights in America. He was not an ideologue. How could he be, when kingmakers from both the

Republican and Democratic parties in California asked him in the early 1970s to be their candidate for the US Senate? That's right, both parties. Both knew his celebrity and resonant voice could persuade an audience to support their policies. He turned both parties down because he loved making films. When he went to work for the NRA, he owned only a few guns. What he had was a passionate belief in every American's rights as given in the Constitution. And the Second Amendment was under threat. So when he roused the gun lobby's faithful to their feet at the NRA's 2000 convention by raising a replica Revolutionary flintlock over his head and declared it could only be taken 'from my cold dead hands,' that dramatizes a gun owner's passion for his right of ownership."

Middleton concluded: "This bill will crush the gun industry and place gun rights on a slippery slope toward confiscation. I ask you to reject it." Applause was sparse.

Bixby spoke last. He looked out across the chamber. "My colleague referenced a Revolutionary-era flintlock in his speech. I also have a prop." He lifted a book high above his head with his right hand. "This is the great novel about Gettysburg, *The Killer Angels*. It won the Pulitzer Prize. After the first day of battle, two Union soldiers are guarding several Confederate prisoners. A boy in blue asks them, 'Why are you fighting?' A Southern boy says, 'For my rats.' The Union soldier is confused. 'Your what?' Again the prisoner says, 'My rats.' Finally, the Union soldier understands. 'Oh, your rights?' The prisoner nods. The Southern boy had finally made himself understood." Bixby set the book down on the lectern. "I've been thinking about the rights the Confederate boys fought for—their state's right to allow slavery. These country boys didn't own slaves. But they were Americans, and Abe Lincoln wasn't going to take their rights away. A Southern plantation owner's economic advantage of labor stolen from slaves cut into the pay of these country boys. But that wasn't a factor. They may not have cared about keeping men and women in bondage. Not a factor. All they knew was that their rights were at risk. Their deep-rooted belief in their individual rights had such power that they were willing to die for these 'rats.' So they soldiered up."

Bixby scanned the room. "Now we know many supporters of the Second Amendment don't own a gun and don't want one. But like Charlton Heston, they believe the Second Amendment is sacred. It's their right as an individual, and rights are pure. This bill we are to vote on says you can keep your guns, let's just hold gun companies liable for illegal and abusive sales practices. It's just one step this country needs to take to cut down on gun violence. But they only hear the word 'infringement.' They don't care about the larger picture, the moral dimension of it."

He glanced around the chamber. "That's two groups of good Americans who'll stand up for their rights. The group years ago allowed humans to be shackled; today's group allows innocent Americans to be murdered by gunfire, at least forty-five people a day, every day last year and this year and next year, until we agree in Washington to do something about it."

He paused to gather his strength, and when he spoke again I saw the power of a nineteenth-century New England preacher thundering condemnation from a pulpit. In an eloquent roar he said, "In every country, to take a life is a crime. To every people, it is evil. The religions of the world teach us that it is a sin. Why, then, are our politics so conflicted over it?"

As the House clerk began the roll-call vote, our group ceased murmuring, but it was not still, for so fixed were our senses on the proceedings that I felt a throbbing of our collective conscience. Our eyes watched the electronic tally board on the wall across from the gallery. Would an opponent of the bill be absent? That would help. I heard Jeffries vote 'Yea,' and I felt a small personal victory. Bixby now had a chance. The vote was even. With only a few votes left, Fletcher Lowell moaned; he was the first to figure Bixby had been beaten. When the clerk announced the final tally, the bill lost by two votes.

Grumbles of disappointment rose throughout the gallery and from the floor. We sat stunned.

Sam Bixby had lost. I had lost.

After a few minutes, it was time to go. People began rising sluggishly to leave. I thought of Jeffries's advice, that a narrow loss meant a bill remained viable. Bixby would try again, and when he did, I hoped that, like Jack waking from a coma and living a long life, Congress would wake up, *wake up*, to the need for this bill and any bill that vastly curbed gun violence. I stood at the top of the steps, and as people passed I said, "We'll get another chance, and next time we'll win." That did little to hearten the group. We gathered on the sidewalk at the designated spot. The buses came up and we climbed on board. Kelly and I found seats in the rear near the scented lavatory. People settled into high-backed seats, and when all rustling died away, the bus was as still as a tomb.

As the driver pulled away for the long ride up the interstate, I felt depressed. Congress had again showed its indifference to mass shootings. I thought about Jack and how happy he had been to make the wrestling team and his confidence that he would contribute to a championship, just as his father had done. What had Dr. Bertrand said, that Jack was improving? It helped, to think that he may also get another chance.

Milton Keynes UK
Ingram Content Group UK Ltd.
UKHW042146281024
450365UK00010B/649